OH MY
Roared

PARANORMAL DATING AGENCY

NEW YORK TIMES and USA TODAY
BESTSELLING AUTHOR

MILLY TAIDEN

Oh, My Roar

Published By: Latin Goddess Press

Winter Springs, FL 32708

http://millytaiden.com

Cover by Willsin Rowe

Edited by: Tina Winograd

Formatting: AG Formatting

OH, MY ROAR

Francesca Virgata wants a mate. She longs for the perfect kind of love her parents had. There's only one problem, she has zero prospects. Thankfully, she's heard of Gerri Wilder who promises to make all her mating dreams come true.

Theo and Marcus are best friends and share everything, even women. So when they both fall for Francesca, it's only natural they have a friendly competition over who can get the girl. After some thought, and a hot little interlude, they realize she shouldn't choose one over the other, they should work together to make the perfect triad. A lion, a tiger and a bear, oh my!

There has been talk of abuse in Francesca's pride and she won't tolerate it. She'll fight tooth and claw to ensure all members are safe. But when her brother turns on her, who will protect her? Theo and Marcus will do anything for her, but it might be easier to let them both go than to choose only one of the men she's come to love.

—For my readers

You curvies rock!

PROLOGUE

Damn, her feet hurt. Gerri knew better than to hike the three-level mall in four-inch heels. But birthday presents must be bought, torture shoes or not. She'd just wear flip-flops the rest of the week—as long as she wasn't meeting clients, anyway.

Shopping bags lying on the kitchen table, Gerri fell into her home office chair and let the cushions suck her into comfort. A good office chair was one of the best things you could buy yourself. Money should go where you spend your time. Some spent it in front of the TV, some traveling, some reading. Gerri spent hers in her office, always on the

1

lookout for another love connection.

She wiggled her mouse to bring her laptop screen to life then logged into her email. She purposely hadn't checked it while shopping and was now paying the price for that little disconnect from the world.

Twenty-five messages awaited her attention. Fortunately, her system automatically pushed spam and junk mail to other folders. Unfortunately, that meant all twenty-five she needed to respond to.

The first three came within seconds of each other. Well, a few people were on the same wavelength. Maybe they needed to be together on more than that.

Francesca Virgata, subject: Please help, 1:12 p.m.

Marcus Ursav, subject: Please help, 1:13 p.m.

Theo Liannus, subject: Help please, 1:14 p.m.

Seems Theo liked to do things backwards. That made her wonder. A sudden image of the three popped into her head and a slow smile curved her lips. Oh, my. These three had no idea what they had coming.

ONE

Francesca and her brother, Shane, sat next to their dad's hospital bed in his nursing home room. He wasn't looking as well as he had last week. Francesca worried the time was coming when they would no longer needed the services of the skilled assistance home.

They lost their mother a long time ago. She had been young and it was hard on them. But losing her father would be devastating. He'd been the grounding aspect in her life. As pride leader of their tiny tiger community, he was more than just Dad to her.

"Now, both of you listen up—" her dad's speech was interrupted by yet another coughing attack.

"Dad, we're not kids anymore," Francesca said. "We'll be fine."

"Yes, I know that's what you think, but when the time comes for you to make decisions, you'll wish I was still there."

"Dad," Shane said, "we'll wish you were there, decisions or not." Francesca couldn't have agreed more.

"Sure, sweet talk me now, children of mine. My final will and testament is completed."

Francesca sighed. She hated when her dad spoke of dying. Sometimes she didn't want to be that grounded. A little head in the clouds was occasionally nice. Her brother, on the other hand, didn't seem to mind.

"Remember what I taught you," he started.

"Yes," Shane said. "The people always come first, right after family. Love is more important than power, and leaders serve others."

Dad beamed with pride. Even though Francesca knew the same lines by heart, being second born, she wasn't destined to rule the pride. She'd have a normal life with a mate and kids. Whenever she found her mate that was. With advances in communications and traveling, finding one's true mate was becoming a more common thing. She so very much wanted to find hers.

But strangely enough, whenever she thought about children, her stomach became nervous and doubt crept into her mind. The only logic she could put to that was children frightened her, which didn't sound very logical. Especially for a female.

But really, she was never around kids except when she was one. She never babysat, so she didn't know how to change a diaper, feed an infant, keep it from crying, how to hold it when it was still all noodley. So much she didn't know. But that wasn't her fault. After school every day, she helped her dad in the tiger pride's office.

Instead of diapers, she learned to change toner cartridges, feed paper to the copy machine, fix the desktop when it froze and crashed. Which ten years later, she was still doing. She sighed and tuned back in to her father talking to Shane.

"Listen when a member complains," Dad said. "There are always two sides to a story and usually a deeper meaning behind problems." Shane nodded and looked deeply entrenched in their father's philosophy. That was why he was heir to the alpha seat. Francesca had no argument with that. Her brother had always been good and nice when they were kids. He even broke up with his girlfriends by giving them flowers.

5

"Don't worry, Dad," Shane said. "You taught me your ethics well. I will make sure our small pride becomes the most respected community around."

Dad patted her brother's hand. "Of that, I'm sure. With your sister running the office, you two will make a great team." She could see her dad's exhaustion coming on.

"Yeah, Dad. We got this," Francesca said. "When you come home, it'll be like you were never gone." He started to say something, but she didn't want to hear him talk about not coming home again. "You're tired, now. Shane and I will see you in a couple days." She leaned down and kissed his cheek. "Love you, Dad. Get some rest."

Francesca climbed into the passenger side of the SUV as Shane got behind the wheel. He looked at his watch. "I'll drop you at the office. I have a meeting soon." It seemed like he was always at meetings anymore. Dad was right when he said she ran the office. Shane was hardly there anymore. But he didn't seem to be bring any business stuff back to the office. No paperwork, no contracts, no clients. Nothing but grumpiness lately.

"You know, Francesca, it's extremely important that our pride grows and becomes a powerhouse. Our survival depends on the next several years."

"Our survival?" she said. "Shane, you sound like Armageddon is coming. Ease up."

"No. We can't ease up. We'll be eaten alive. Bullied. We must become stronger than Dad has ever imagined. I see the future. I know what has to be done. We all have to sacrifice."

"Sacrifice?" She didn't like the way her brother was starting to sound. "Shane, what are you talking about? Who has to sacrifice what?"

His brows furrowed and lips pressed together. When he noticed her watching him, he turned away from her.

"Shane?" she started. "What the hell was the whole conversation with Dad? He never said anything about sacrificing. What are you saying?"

"I'm talking about our pride needing to stand out to protect itself in these times. If you don't, you'll get run over by the big guys and wiped out. The more powerful you are, the safer you are."

Where did he get those ideas? "No. Dad said living an honest life—"

"Dad isn't part of the modern world, Francesca. It's up to you and me to take the pride into the next generation."

"I agree, but we're not doing anything stupid, are we?" When he said nothing, she pushed him. "Are we?"

"No, we're doing what's necessary," he said.

Luckily for him, her phone buzzed indicating an email came in. She pulled her cell from the front of her purse and clicked the mail app. The email at the top of her list was from GerriWilder@GetMeAMate.

Francesca:

Thank you for reaching out to me.

I am having an informal get-together at Ruth's Chris Steak House. Please join me for cocktails and steak hors d'oeuvres at 6 p.m. tomorrow night.

Gerri

TWO

"Marcus Ursav," his mom yelled across the backyard, "get your furry behind over here and pick up your niece. She's headed for the mud puddle." His older sister sprinted from a group of relatives gathered around the grill.

"No, no, baby girl," she hollered. "No muddy water! Marcus, you suck as a babysitter."

"I'm not babysitting," he said. "You're the mom." He may have sounded disgusted, but in reality, he loved all his nieces and nephews. They were the highlights of his Wednesday nights.

When he moved out of his parents' home a few years ago, they became empty nesters.

Even though they said they loved their new lifestyle, Mom insisted all siblings come over on Wednesday nights for dinner. No excuses. And being a weeknight, he had no excuse. Well, any night, he had no excuse since he had no life.

Working as a forensic accountant on a freelance basis wasn't too exciting. For a spectator, it was like watching paint dry. You sit and stare at a computer monitor or ledgers for hours. But for him, finding the one link in a thousand entries that tied a criminal to the deed was a natural high. He was very good at what he did and often worked high profile IRS cases.

But Wednesday nights were always for family. And his dad grilled a kick-ass steak. Plus, being the only sibling not mated, he got to take leftovers home. When there were leftovers. Seemed like every few months, another small, furry muzzle joined the table.

He longed for his own small, furry muzzles. But finding a mate came first. And that was where the problem started. Working from home did not allow for socializing or getting out of the house much.

If not for his roommate, Theo, he'd gone crazy a long time ago, and the fridge would've always been empty. Theo was his link to the world after he'd spent days and nights locked in his home office trying to take down white-collar crooks.

Sudden commotion around the grill caught his eye. Several people, including Mom, was helping Dad sit at the picnic table. Dad made loud sucking-wind noises. His COPD breathing disorder got worse every year. His long time job as a firefighter did him no favors. Medication helped, but didn't cure.

Marcus scooped up a nephew, this one in bear form with a diaper, and sat at the table with his father.

"Here, Dad," Marcus said, "hold Karsten." The little bear shifted and reached for Paw Paw. He watched as the little one snuggled into his father's neck and chest. His heart hurt for his own offspring.

"Got yourself a mate yet?" Dad asked.

Marcus slumped, his elbows propped on the table. "No, Dad. I don't have time to date or anything."

"Yeah," his father said, "I don't have a lot of time, either, and would like to see some cubs from you."

"Dad." Marcus frowned. He didn't want to think about his father dying. The old man was too young. "You'll be glad to hear I've contacted a mate consultant to help me find someone."

Dad raised a brow. "A mate consultant?"

"Yeah, she's going to find a mate I'm compatible with," he said.

"Compatible?" his father asked. "What about love?" He leaned closer to him. "And she has to be good in the sack. You gotta sleep with her before you marry, you know."

"Harry!" his mom hollered, making them both wince, "I heard that."

"I know you did, dear," Dad said loudly. "And you're still damn hot. My bear will take you right now on this table."

Cries of ewww and gross came from the siblings and in-laws. The kids giggled at everyone's sudden reactions. Mom smiled and winked at Dad. The love was definitely there after all these years. That's what he wanted.

The cell phone tucked in his back pocket beeped, informing him of an incoming email. After pulling it out and thumbing the passcode, he saw an email from GerriWilder@GetMeAMate.

Marcus:

Thank you for reaching out to me.

I am having an informal get-together at Ruth's Chris Steak House. Please join me for cocktails and steak hors d'oeuvres at 6 p.m. tomorrow night.

OH, MY ROARED

Gerri

THREE

Theo tore open the utility bill his roommate, Marcus, set on the kitchen table earlier. Theodor Liannus, Apt. 212. Every time he looked at his address, he was reminded of the vast amount of land and forest he'd inherited but could do nothing with at the moment. It was expensive to build and maintain a house. Not to mention, it'd be only himself. So he opted to remain here with Marcus.

Long ago, his parents and brother were killed in a tragic car accident. He would've died also if not for a firefighter who braved the burning car to pull him out seconds before it blew up. That event had more impact on his life than he would've ever thought. His career as a firefighter and first responder was about the only thing that mattered to him. Besides Marcus and his family.

The fireman who saved him was Marcus's father. After that devastating night, Marcus's family became his, too. Throughout their school years, the two boys were inseparable. Their first dates, they doubled.

Even without the words, they seemed to always know how the other was feeling: down from losing a ballgame, to orgasmic highs during sex. He'd never forget how they figured out they could sense each other.

During summer break of their senior year, Marcus was at his girlfriend's house, with her parents away. Theo was at his girlfriend's house where the family was grilling out by the pool. While sitting next to his girlfriend and her mom on loungers poolside, he got a raging boner for no reason.

He snatched up a towel and put it over his lap. His swim trunks were long and baggy, but being a bear shifter, the material still didn't hide as much as he'd like. At that moment, his girl's dad decided it was time for an impromptu game of basketball while the steaks finished up.

Theo was horrified. How would it look with him having a huge hard-on while sitting with his girlfriend's mom? He feigned injury to his knee and claimed he was hungry. So they sat on the porch gathered around the table.

As he chewed his first bite of meat, an incredible feeling rolled through him, making him moan. The three at the table stared at him. The only thing he could do was say the steak was the best he'd ever had, even though slightly burnt. He suppressed a couple other urges to groan, somewhat, and excused himself for the restroom. By himself, he jerked-off to relieve the pressure. After that, the girlfriend's dad never grilled steaks again.

When he and Marcus were at home that night, they shared stories and realized what had happened. They never told anyone, not because they were embarrassed, but because they knew something special was between them. Plus, it was no one else's business anyway.

They worked on blocking, both sending and receiving, to cut back on potentially disastrous public exhibitions. Now, it came second nature to keep everything inside him, inside. He'd learned to control his emotions in all situations. And being a firefighter and first responder challenged that daily.

But that also inhibited him when it came to showing emotions to females he had interest in. All his relationships ended with the same claim: he couldn't open up to her, wouldn't share his feelings with her. And they were right.

He laid the paper bill on the table and scrounged around the kitchen for food. He'd forgotten it was Wednesday night and that Marcus would be with the fam. When he wasn't working nightshift, he was there, too, considered as one of the siblings.

When one of the new guys hired on, Theo made a deal with him so the guy could go home at night to see his kids and wife. It wasn't like Theo had anyone at home waiting for him. No skin off his back. Good thing was it kept him from getting down being alone at night. Alone except for Marcus, but he didn't count. Neither had any desire for sex with the other. Sharing a woman was fine, but they weren't sexually interested in each other.

But sex with a female would be great. A feline shifter would hit the spot even better. That way his lion got something out of the connection. His other half took that opportunity to inform him that, at this point, it'd been so long, he'd take just about anything breathing. He'd prefer their mate, but wouldn't be picky.

Yeah, yeah. He got it. They'd just have to wait. Hopefully, the email he sent earlier to a matchmaker would turn out fruitful. They'd see.

Bowl of cereal in hand, he sat on a barstool in front of his laptop. He logged on to check out his email. One looked particularly interesting. He double clicked on it. It was from a GerriWilder@GetMeAMate.

Theo:

Thank you for reaching out to me.

I am having an informal get-together at Ruth's Chris Steak House. Please join me for cocktails and steak hors d'oeuvres at 6 p.m. tomorrow night.

Gerri

FOUR

Francesca brushed her hands down the front of her skirt, flattening the non-existent wrinkles. She spun away from the restaurant's front door and stepped away. Her hands rubbed over each other. Good god. What was wrong with her? It wasn't like she had to marry or mate some stranger she met here. It was just a meet and greet kinda thing.

In the time she'd paced the sidewalk to the entrance, several men and women, each alone, each a shifter, had entered. She wasn't the only one there. Her tigress was about ready to call her a pussy and push her inside. The animal wasn't a pansy in a group of unknown people. Right, Francesca thought, it was more like the tigress caught a whiff of cooking meat when the door opened.

Didn't matter, she had to get inside.

Fine, she'd go in. Francesca sucked in a deep breath, lifted her chin and boobs, and strutted through the door. The huge drop in lighting took her human eyes a minute to get used to, but her tigress saw perfectly in its ideal environment.

Francesca saw the bar and hurried across the floor toward an empty stool. "Vodka, on the rocks, please," she said. Her animal grimaced. Really? Yes, really. She downed the clear liquid and realized she'd yet not taken another breath since entering. Shit, she needed to chill out.

A heavenly aroma floated to her noise. She closed her eyes and let it roll through her.

"Excuse me." An even heavenlier voice spoke in her ear. Deep, rumbly, scrumptious. She turned on her stool to see a gorgeous dark blond surfer boy meeting her eyes. Holy fuck was he stunning. Under his white T-shirt, she noted powerful shoulders and thick biceps that led to rounded forearms. Who would've thought forearms were sexy?

She saw his smirk at her checking him out and felt heat build in her cheeks. This was why she didn't want to come in. She knew she'd embarrass herself, and she did it within the first few minutes of arrival. Great. If the guy didn't smell so damn good, her tigress would've walked off and found a cushy place to sleep.

His smile turned genuine with her rosy cheeks. "I apologize, ma'am. I didn't mean to startle you."

Startled? Yeah, that's what happened. He startled her. His eyes remained on hers. Then she realized he was waiting for her to say something. But what? Her mouth opened then closed. She smiled for lack of anything else coming to mind.

"I wondered," he said, "how the vodka is tonight. It's my drink of choice, as long as it's smooth."

Vodka? What vodka? The one you just inhaled.

Francesca sat straighter. "I apologize," she finally said. "I just arrived and hadn't gotten my bearings yet." She held her hand out. "I'm Francesca Virgata."

His large hand encompassed hers, work-calloused fingers rubbing her skin, sending goose bumps up her arms. "I'm Theo Liannus." Her cat told her he was a lion. Yeah, buddy. Big, bad lion dick swinging in the air would be good. Pumping in her would

21

be better.

Theo sniffed deeply and coughed out a choke.

Francesca crossed her leg over another and bowed her head, trying to control her tigress's reaction to the lion. "Nice to meet you, Theo. My tigress is also thrilled, if you hadn't noticed."

His brows bent. "Noticed?" His throat cleared. "No, I didn't smell a thing."

She couldn't help but laugh at his obvious lie to save her, yet another, embarrassing moment. His surfer boy hair slid forward, covering one of his dark eyes. His smile warmed her heart. He was gorgeous everywhere. From the waist up, anyway.

"Back to my question," he said.

"Oh," she shook her head, "of course. The vodka is very good. I might even have another."

"Let me." Theo lifted two fingers at the bartender, who nodded. A second later another glass with ice sat next to hers. That was a thoughtful gesture from him, but it was an open bar, so... He lifted his tumbler. "To new friends."

Francesca smiled and raised her glass. "Yes, to new friends." She sipped her drink then set it in front of her. She gave a silent sigh. She was so bad at making conversation or small talk. She'd spent a majority of her free time working in the office growing up, and now the art form was lost on her. If they weren't talking timesheets, expenses, or scheduling, she didn't have a clue what to say.

To her surprise, Theo settled on the stool next to her. "So, Francesca, what do you do for a living?"

His amazing scent encompassed her. If she could just sit here and breathe him in, she'd die happy. "I work in the office of my pride's prime. He's my dad, actually."

"Really? I wouldn't have pegged you as an alpha female."

Of course, he wouldn't. She could barely speak more than three words at a time. She'd blushed twice in two minutes and was having a second drink in as many minutes. He probably thought she was a lush and would be easy.

He jerked in his chair. "No! That's not what I meant." He wiped a hand over his face. "Let me rephrase." He sighed. "I meant you don't seem like a stuck-up bitch who thinks others should bow at her feet."

She laughed at his explanation. "You got me there. I definitely don't think others should bow to me or anyone. Unless you're

23

the Pope or something." He laughed with her. "What do you do, Theo?"

"I'm a firefighter. My house is #22. I live on the west side not far from there."

"Wow." Francesca was honestly impressed. Firefighting was a dangerous job. He could die any day. How would she feel dating someone who could be gone in a heartbeat? Her eyes lifted, meeting his. Breath caught in her throat.

She saw a fire of his own there. Then a twinkle of gold. Was that his lion? Was it interested in her and her tiger? Her heart sped out of control. He leaned closer, licking his lips. Did he want to kiss her already? Was she okay with that? Hell yes! Her shot of vodka must've kicked in.

Then a loud beeping sound turned all heads at the bar toward them. Theo sat back and pushed a button on his watch. "Sorry 'bout that. I need to head to the fire house for my shift." Her heart fell. She finally found someone who interested her tiger and herself. He tossed back the rest of his drink.

"Uh, Francesca," he started, "would you like to go to a show with me Sunday afternoon? I have great tickets and would really like to see you again."

She smiled. "I'd love to go with you." She pulled her phone out. "What's your number?

24

I'll call you." She added his info and saved it.

Theo scooped up her hand. "It was fantastic meeting you, Francesca. I hate leaving such a beautiful creature as you, but I have cats and children to save." He winked. His antics made her laugh. "Until later, milady." He kissed the back of her hand and then walked out the door.

FIVE

Marcus straightened his tie and hurried inside the steak house. He'd gotten so involved in his current project, he lost track of time. If it wasn't for his bladder reminding him he needed to take a break, he might have missed the entire event.

Theo left the apartment a while ago, going to some event he was rather secretive about. Which was somewhat normal for Theo. Ever since that one time in high school when Marcus went to his girlfriend's house when her parents were away and had sex, Theo kept his love life to himself. Not that his roommate had much of a life. Had about as much as he had, which was non-existent. That was why he emailed Gerri Wilder, hoping her services would help him find someone to share his life with. And get his family off his back about a mate.

Stepping inside, the low light had him stopping for a second. Several people in the small restaurant mingled or sat at the bar talking to others of the opposite sex. If he was correct, it looked like the entire restaurant was reserved for their party. Wow. That was a pretty penny.

"Marcus, Marcus Ursav." He looked around for the female calling his name. A tall woman in a business suit and high-heeled shoes waved at him. How did she walk in those things? Very gracefully. It seemed like she floated over the floor on her way to him. "Marcus, I'm Gerri Wilder." She held her hand out. "It's a pleasure to meet you."

Ah, yes. He recognized her from her photo on her website. He took her hand. "The pleasure is mine, Ms. Wilder."

"Please," she replied, "call me Gerri. I insist." She turned to face the crowd. "Thank you for coming. I was worried you wouldn't be able to make it when I saw Theo alone."

He was surprised the woman knew he and Theo were friends. But she might've talked with his roommate and learned from him. Yet, she knew who he was and he'd not sent a picture with his email.

"I must say," Gerri said, "I'm flattered that

such a highly successful professional as yourself would ask for my help. You have quite a prolific online presence with the accounting sites."

Granted, he'd given interviews for online magazines, contributed to a few blogs, and had articles here and there on certain cases he worked. But prolific? Maybe he should check that out. He'd never googled his own name before. Probably a good idea.

"Really," he replied, "I'm flattered that someone of your reputation would have time for such a sorry case of mateless-ness as I."

Gerri joined with him in a chuckle and wrapped her arm around his, guiding him forward. "Nonsense, Marcus. I find great satisfaction in helping those who help others. What comes around, goes around, wouldn't you agree?"

He felt she had an underlying meaning, but didn't know what it was. "Yes, it's nice to think those who do good, or evil, get that returned to them in spades."

She smiled. "I'm glad you agree. Oh, look." She aimed him toward the side of the bar. "Here's someone I'd like you to meet."

Sitting on a stool was the most beautiful woman he'd ever seen. His bear lifted its head and took a whiff. Yeah, baby, this night was looking up. And to think the bear

28

thought about hibernating the next few months until his human's current bad guys were caught.

"Francesca," Gerri said.

The gorgeous woman on the stool looked at his escort, then him, and smiled. He and his bear turned into putty. How he got the next twenty feet to the stunning lady, he didn't remember.

"Ms. Wilder," she said. Her voice was as calming as waves washing on the beach. "I recognize you from your website. You're even prettier in person."

Gerri's hand lay on her chest. "Thank you, dear. You are too kind." The women chitchatted a bit more, but it became a buzz in his mind as he tried unsuccessfully not to stare. Then he heard his name. "Marcus, this is Francesca Virgata."

His hand floated forward. He hoped his bear was in control because he sure wasn't. When his hand touched hers, electricity zapped him. His bear jumped into a victory dance. This was her, the one.

He really needed to chill out. They needed to impress her first. If they came across as stupid, their chances were nil. Don't say anything dumb.

"Hi, Francesca. You're more beautiful than

I could've ever imagined." That wasn't what his animal had in mind for a first line.

The woman's eyes widened and her checks blushed, making her that much more perfect.

Gerri looked over her shoulder. "Oh, look. There's someone I need to talk to. You kids have a great time." She leaned into Marcus. "You've got this." She walked away and was quickly out of his mind.

Marcus snapped out of his haze, realizing he was "alone" with this woman—Francesca. He needed to fix his creepy image before she walked away, too.

"Francesca, I apologize for sounding like a freak. I was caught off guard when Gerri...when she..." His bear groaned and dropped its muzzle into its paws. Might as well head off to hibernate now and miss the humiliation coming.

The lovely Francesca laughed. Maybe he'd stick around a bit longer.

"When Gerri introduced you, is that what you're trying to say?" she responded.

His face flushed hot. "That's it. I'm not good at this meeting others kinda thing." At least he was honest. The wonderful laugh came again.

"No worries. I'm horrible at it, too." She

30

motioned at the stool next to her. "Would you like to sit?"

"Yeah, that'd be great." He hopped up on the seat and signaled the barkeep. "I'll have a water..." he turned to her, "what are you drinking?" He glanced at the clear liquid in her glass.

"Water." She smiled. Nice, he thought. They were compatible with drinks. His bear snorted. Right, you and seven billion other humans on the planet who drink water.

"Have you been here long?" he asked, hoping to get a conversation going.

"I arrived shortly after the party started." She leaned closer to him. "Actually, I got here well before time, but had to work my nerve up to come in, which took a bit." She was so adorable.

"If I hadn't been running late, I would've done the same thing. Fortunately, with rushing in, I didn't have to stop and think what I was really doing. That helped." She laughed with him.

"Did you work late?" she asked.

"I did. I started a new project today and got too wrapped up in it. Lost track of time," he admitted.

"That's great you like what you do so much that time slips by. I'm mostly the opposite. I love talking with the people who come into the office, but the work itself, the same things over and over, gets monotonous."

"What kind of office is it? Lawyer, doctor's?" he asked.

"My dad's the prime for a tiger pride nearby and my brother and I help him keep everything running smoothly."

His smile widened. "I knew you were an alpha female. I could tell by the quiet authority you hold yourself with." She looked a bit taken aback. His smile faded. "I don't mean anything negative by that. It's stunning—you're stunning to watch."

Her rosy cheeks returned. "It's not that. Someone recently told me they would've never thought I was an alpha."

He scooped up her hand and brought it to his lips. "That person must be a moron then. You glow self-assurance." He kissed her hand. She smelled so good. Like fresh baked bread. Strange, but that was what he scented.

She laughed a little louder than before. "Maybe he was. Who knows?" Her eyes settled on his. A twinkle flashed in her pupils. Was that her tiger, coming out to take a peek? His bear showed further interest in her. Yup, time to mate.

Whoa! Marcus wanted to kick his bear at the moment. He and Francesca continued talking and laughing and ordering more water from the bartender. He knew she liked him by the way her eyes sparkled for him. At least he hoped that's what she was feeling. When he looked up, he noted a lot of couples had formed. The next time he looked up, almost everyone was gone.

Gerri set two fresh glasses of water before them. "Last call for the hard stuff." She smiled from behind the bar.

Francesca looked around, alarmed. "Are we the last ones here?"

"No worries, dear," Gerri said. "Just setup a date for this weekend and Marcus will walk you to your car." She winked at them both. "Have a good evening." She walked away, leaving Marcus ready to have a cow. He wanted to ask her out, but was scared shitless of her rejecting him. Wouldn't be anything new. Just get it over with.

"Uh, Francesca," he mumbled, running a shaky hand through his hair. She looked at him with a sly grin.

"Marcus, I'd love to go out with you Saturday."

He sat straighter and sucked in a breath. "You would? I mean, that's great. Here," he handed his phone to her, "text your phone from mine and we'll both have each other's number."

He walked her out to her car. She belonged to him now. She was his mate. And he would take care of her and make her the happiest woman on the planet because she made him the happiest man.

SIX

Marcus poured his first cup of coffee and reclined on the sofa, watching the sun come over the adjacent buildings. One thing he missed about living with his parents was their rural location. No tall buildings blocking the view, no cars honking or polluting the air. Just peace and smaller critters romping through the forests out back. He'd love to get back to that. He could literally work from anywhere, as long as he had Internet, he could live in Antarctica.

His bear shivered. Maybe not there. How about a nudist beach where it could run around naked? His animal must've been high. The damn thing didn't wear clothes. High on love.

Marcus would agree with that. They'd

found their mate and now they had to woo her to make sure she knew they wanted her, and only her, now and forever.

He heard the elevator down the hall ding then a moment later, Theo opened the door. Was he humming? Theo never hummed or whistled. He did occasionally belt out AC/DC in the shower. Those were times Marcus prayed the hot water would run out before he did.

"Hey, what's up, Marcus? You are," he said and laughed at his own joke. "Get it? You're up—out of bed—"

"Yeah, Theo, I get it. Why're you in such a good mood?"

He came around the sofa and plopped down, almost causing Marcus to spill his coffee. "I found her, man."

"Her, who?" Marcus asked.

"Her, the one, dude. My mate. I met her at a party last night." He laid his head back and spread his arms. "She's so beautiful."

"I thought you worked last night."

"I did. At least, I think I did. I couldn't think of anything else but her. Fortunately, it was quiet all night. No calls."

Marcus wondered if Theo's finding his mate and him finding his own on the same night was one of those strange connections they had since kids.

Theo looked at him. "What's wrong? Why aren't you happy for me?" His eyes widened. "This doesn't mean I'm kicking you out. Well, maybe it does. No. She'll be with me in my room. You'll be fine."

"That's a hell no, I'm not listening to your headboard bang against the wall all night, every night," Marcus grumped.

"Okay," Theo placated, "I'll get rid of the headboard. I never liked it anyway."

"No, Theo," Marcus said. "That's not the point."

"What is the point?" he asked. Marcus sat up on the couch and put his feet on the floor.

"I found my mate last night, too."

Theo stared at him. "I didn't know you left the house. Did she deliver a pizza or something?" He breathed in heavily, probably searching for that special day-after pizza smell.

"No, I was invited to a meet and greet by a mate consultant."

"A what?" Theo asked.

"Someone to help me find a mate." Didn't anyone but him not understand mate consultant?

"You're gonna sleep with the chick

37

beforehand, right, dude?" Theo looked concerned.

"God, Theo. You're just like my dad. That's the first thing he said." Marcus stood from the sofa to get more coffee.

His roommate smiled. "I was trained by the best."

Marcus rolled his eyes. "Sometimes I think you should've been born into the family and I was the pseudo-adopted one."

"Aw, come on, man. Don't hate me 'cause I'm beautiful."

Good god. Marcus would've shot coffee out his nose had any been in his mouth. "Whatever, dude. You and your sissy surfer hair," he teased.

"Hey, man. You carry a hundred pounds of equipment up twenty floors and see how sissy you are." Theo had a point. Marcus wasn't much for the athletic stuff, even though he kept in good shape. His sedentary lifestyle called for him to work out at the gym or die of heart disease at age thirty.

"Okay," Marcus conceded, "I'm thrilled you found your mate last night." A horrible thought crossed his mind. Please god, no. "Theo, where was your party last night?"

"Some place pretty spiffy. Ruth's steakhouse or something." Marcus groaned.

This was not happening. "Why? Steak kabobs were great. Still moo-ing."

"Does your mate have long brown hair that looks like flowing silk?" Marcus asked.

"Yeah, it's beautiful. I can't wait to fist my hand in it while she sucks me down." A shudder rippled through his friend's body. "Does yours, too?"

He chose not to answer as he filled his coffee mug. "Does she have a curvy body that would feel great pressed under you?"

"And an ass that doesn't quit. I've always liked asses. I'm an ass man, through and through." Theo rubbed his crotch and he stretched on the sofa.

Marcus mumbled, "Was that 'ass, man' or 'ass-man'?" He shook his head. "Maybe just ass would be correct."

"What are saying in there, dude?" Theo continued to rub his dick while Marcus leaned against the encased opening between the kitchen and living space.

"Is her name Francesca Virgata?"

Theo's hand and body froze on the sofa. His eyes narrowed. "How did you know that?" For fuck's sake! Marcus turned back to the kitchen as Theo jumped off the couch. "You been spying on me? What the hell? Did one of the guys from the station call you?"

Marcus plopped onto a chair at the table. "Fuck me. No, I'm not spying and no one called. The woman I met last night was Francesca Virgata. And I thought she was into me."

"Fuck you is right. She was heavy into me. And she's mine. I saw her first."

"That's only because you had to go to work, so you left before I did." Another thought hit him. "And why didn't you tell me you were going to the get-together?"

Theo sputtered without an answer, then spit out, "Why didn't you tell me you were going?"

"Really, Theo?" Marcus said. "Answering a question with a question is lame."

"Politicians get away with it. So can I," he replied.

"All right, enough." With both hands, Marcus scratched through his messy morning hair. "We need to figure this out."

"There's nothing to figure out. I saw her first." Theo crossed his arms over his chest.

Marcus glared at him. "We aren't in second grade, Theo."

"I know, but it worked for me then." Marcus almost laughed at his roomie's pouting.

"Because I backed off so you could play with Marissa Caders. Then two days later, you didn't like her anymore."

"She was boring. All she wanted was to sit on the merry-go-round and make me push it." He shook his head. "Did you see her throw up on my shoes?"

Marcus leaned back in his chair and laughed. He'd forgotten that part. "No, but I smelled them all the way home." He slapped a hand on the table. "I told you, you were pushing her too fast. But did you listen to me? Noooo. You got what you deserved."

"Whatever, man." Theo crossed to the fridge, plucked a chocolate milk from the door and unscrewed the top. "You know," he said as he closed the fridge, "we could make a bet to see who gets her."

Marcus dropped his head back and stared at the ceiling. "No wonder you're still single," he said. "Haven't you seen every movie where the guys make a bet, then she finds out and they both get dumped? Sorry, bro. Ain't dumb enough to fall for that."

"Damn," Theo whispered, "I had to try, at least." He smiled when Marcus raised his brows at him.

"We're handling this like adult men. That is if you can pretend to be one long enough." Marcus eyeballed his best friend across the table. Theo slapped a hand on his chest.

"That hurts. Cuts me deep, man," he pointed to his chest, "right here."

Marcus smirked. "Well, if you die, she's mine."

Theo frowned. "Not funny, dude. Don't go messin' with my mate."

Marcus sighed. "I'm guessing you asked her out."

"Yeah, on Sunday," he said.

Marcus covered his mouth with his hand. He would not laugh out loud at his friend. "You can't seriously be taking her to that?"

Theo's brow raised. "And what are you planning with her?"

"Another question with a question."

Theo growled and waved a hand in the air. "Just answer it."

"If you must know," Marcus sat straighter, "I'm taking her to the outdoor theatre to see Shakespeare's *A Midsummer Night's Dream*."

Theo covered his mouth, Marcus was certain, to imitate his action. "You do that. Come Sunday night, we'll see who she prefers."

Marcus sighed. He hoped this didn't mean an end to their friendship after so many years. But significant others were reasons friends no longer remain friends. He didn't want that.

"I need to get some sleep," Theo said. "Normal shift tonight." He gave a chin pop. "See you then."

"Yeah, have a good rest," Marcus replied. After his roommate's bedroom door closed, he picked up his phone and placed an order.

SEVEN

Francesca sized up the enemy in front of her. He was quite a bit taller, but that was only because she was vertically challenged. She wouldn't let a silly thing like that be the reason she got the shit beat out of her. Nope, not this morning. After such a wonderful evening the night before, she was psyched beyond belief.

She and her opponent circled each other, neither had a hand raised. No weapons had been pulled. No, not for this fight. This would be all skill.

He lunged toward her, fist aimed at her. Easily, she blocked the oncoming missile with her forearm, grabbed his wrist and thrust him to the floor using his own momentum against him. He sprang to his feet. She got lucky on that one.

His eyes flared. It was probably hard for a man to take getting their ass kicked by a woman. A short one at that. Circling again, she focused on his stance. There were telltale signs throughout the body that foretold what was coming.

Fists and biceps relaxed. He wasn't thinking of an upper body punch. His posture straightened just slightly, prepping his core muscles. He'd decided on a lower strike position. But which one? A roundhouse, side strike, hook? His weight shifted onto his left leg. Roundhouse, then.

His right leg bent and lifted at his side, readying to snap around and deliver a foot to her chest. But seeing his muscles prep the move, she was ready. While his leg was in the air, she dropped into a crouch, then swung her leg around to take out his knee and his ability to walk again. An inch before making contact, she stopped all movement.

Point!

Those sitting around the mat lying on the wood floor jumped up and cheered. She and her contestant rushed to their feet and bowed. The sensei dismissed the group for the night's lesson.

Francesca fell back on the mat, exhausted. Who the hell had the brilliant idea to train for a black belt? Oh, right. That was her wanting to teach self-defense to the females in the pride. She must've been high when she filled out the paperwork. Her antagonist, Ben, offered a hand up.

"You're getting good, Francesca," he said. "Being short really helps on those low-to-the-ground movements." She grabbed his hand.

"Thanks, smart ass. I mean, Ben." Her shit-eating-grin matched his. "Your sky-high, praying mantis legs are hard to miss."

He yanked up a white pant leg of his gi showing his thin, hairy limb. "These are rather sexy, aren't they?"

"If you shaved them, we could at least see some skin then, you gorilla," one of the other guys hollered.

"I can't help if I was born this way. Talk to my mom," he yelled back.

"Yeah," joked the other guy, "I'll talk to your mom. After I do her." Francesca rolled her eyes and headed for the lockers. Guys could be so crude sometimes. Actually, most of the time. How was she blessed with so many as company?

After changing into street clothes, she came across Sensei Steve standing outside the small office, hands on his hips.

"Sensei, is everything all right?" she

asked.

"Oh, Francesca," he laid a hand over his chest pocket and both pants pockets, "I seemed to have locked my keys in the office." He pointed through a window. Sure enough, on the corner of the wood desk lay a ring of keys.

She'd never picked a lock before, but it seemed like everyone on TV could do it with two picks. Of course, MacGyver just needed a piece of gum. After googling instructions on her phone, she called on her tigress for a couple long claws. Within a few minutes, the lock popped open. She couldn't believe it. That seemed easy. No wonder everyone could do it.

"Thank you, young lady," Sensei Steve said.

"You're welcome. Looks like I learned more than I intended this morning." She adjusted her purse on her shoulder. "If that's it, then I'll be on my way."

"Francesca," her sensei replied, "may I have a few moments with you?" He fingered the scar on the side of his face that had been there before she was born. It had faded with age, but whenever he worried about something, he always rubbed it. She never asked how he got it. It looked as if it was somewhat prominent at one time.

"Sure." She walked through the door he held open. "What can I do for you?"

Steve closed the door and pulled the blind down. "Francesca, I'm disturbed by things I'm seeing here in the pride."

Whoa. She didn't see this coming. "What kind of things?" she asked.

He sat back in his office chair and sighed. "Francesca, since your father's absence, I've noticed..." he paused. "I fear some of the young men may have become aggressive."

Another shock. "Oh." She thought through her last couple of weeks. Being stuck in the office all the time, she was out of the loop on the community. "Like how?"

"I've not seen anything myself, but several of the younger ladies have enquired about self-defense classes recently. More than ever before. And with things like this, I find there is usually a reason behind the enquiries."

So he hadn't seen anything personally. Maybe he was getting a bit paranoid in his older years. "Thank you for sharing your concerns with me, Sensei. I will discuss this with my brother."

He nodded. "That's all I can ask. How is your father doing?"

"He's doing well. Thank you for asking. Some days are better than others," she answered.

He sighed. "Ever since your mother passed away, he's not been the same. He truly loved her. We all did."

Now she felt awkward talking about her deceased mother. She really loved her mom, too. But being Mom's sibling, he had a right to express himself.

"And what about you, grasshopper? Any love interests? Your father would want you happily mated soon. With him being ill, and one of my closest friends, I feel like I should keep an eye on you and your brother."

She wanted to tell her sensei that she and her brother were old enough to care for themselves, but she understood the need to protect for others, especially someone who never found a mate or had children of their own to love. "Thank you, Uncle Steve. I very much appreciate all you do for us and the community. And I have two dates this weekend."

"Two? Well then, you don't need any help, sounds like." He winked and rose from his chair, grabbed his keys off the desk, and motioned for her to walk out with him. "I know you and your brother are capable of watching yourselves, but I still worry. Can't help it."

She kissed him on the cheek. "You're the

best, Uncle Sensei. I'll see you next lesson." She headed for her car in the morning sunlight as he locked the main doors and watched her drive away.

His words about the guys in the community troubled her. She hadn't witnessed any aggressive actions toward anyone, and none of the ladies shared anything with her. She thought they would since she'd known all of them since she was old enough to recognize faces.

She didn't know what to do.

EIGHT

Sitting at the one stoplight in the little town, Francesca pulled her phone from her purse. Her screen showed she had two text messages waiting. She tapped for the first.

Good morning, beautiful. Just letting you know I'm thinking about you. Looking forward to Saturday. Marcus

Aww, how sweet. She texted back a thank you and similar regards. When she first saw him last night with Gerri, she hadn't seen anyone as gorgeous since...Theo had left ten minutes before.

How could she be so attracted to two men, and at the same time? She'd gone years without one guy turning her head, then in

51

one night, two cause her whiplash. Then stupidly, she agreed to both dates. When did she become one of those women? One thing was for sure, she didn't want to string anyone along. She'd figure out which she liked, if either, and then let the other one go.

The message definitely added points for Marcus.

She went back to the messenger home screen and clicked the other text.

Good morning, gorgeous. Hope your day is great. I can't wait to see you again Sunday. Get ready for a wild ride. Theo

Oh, shit. Now the guys were tied for points. Was it going to be like this until she made her decision? She sighed and replied similar to Marcus's. It'd been a long time since anyone made a fuss over her. Her mom was the designated daughter spoiler and since it was just Dad now, she was not only not spoiled, but barely had attention from anyone.

She wasn't a needy princess by any means. But knowing and being shown she was loved made her feel good about herself. That was hard to find in a world so demanding of everyone's time.

She didn't know what to do here, either. God, she felt like a failure right now.

A car honked and Francesca snapped her head up. The light had turned green. She tossed her phone on the passenger seat and continued toward the office. Thank goodness it was Friday. She wasn't sure if she could last one more day.

After unlocking the office door, turning on all the lights, and starting the extra-large coffeemaker, she dialed into the office voicemail and took down messages community members left last night. A moment later, the front door opened and a delivery man rolled in a hand dolly stacked with boxes.

"I'm looking for Francesca Virgata."

Her brows raised. "That's me." Two more people walked in, all wearing the same uniform the deliver guy wore. And rolling in their own hand dollies. He handed her a clipboard with a form for her to sign.

"We'll get these set up and be out of your hair in a few moments."

Francesca watched as boxes popped open, each holding their own container of flowers. As the man promised, in a few moments, every flat space in the front office had flowers and plants on it. She had her own flower shop. A card sat on the desk in front of her.

Even a room full of flowers isn't nearly as beautiful as you. Marcus

When the visitors closed the door behind them, she stared around the room, awed. Then she sneezed, and sneezed again. Frantic to stop the allergy attack she felt coming, she dug in her purse for her medication. Swallowing a couple pills, she sat back and grabbed a box of tissues. She loved the sentiment, but her watery eyes and sneezing would not be fun.

Time to get working. She pulled the checks from the post office envelopes she picked up on her way. She needed to have them entered into the system and ready for deposit when her brother, Shane, got in.

They'd worked out a while back how to split office responsibilities. Since she did so much computer and paperwork, Shane did all the tasks that required leaving the office. That worked fine with her. If she had to leave, she'd never get done what she needed to.

When she ran the envelope opener under the first flap, the front door opened again. This time a lady she'd never seen before entered.

"Hi," she said, "I'm looking for Francesca Virgata."

Not again. "Are you delivering flowers?" Francesca asked.

The lady smiled. "No. Something much better. Chocolate." Outside, behind the woman standing in the doorway, a van backed up to the front door. Oh god.

By the time this group walked out, Francesca had never seen so much chocolate in one place. Even the Hershey Bar store. She had no idea there were so many varieties, either. Again, she sat back in awe. Another card lay on her desk.

Nothing is as sweet as you, but I thought I'd give it a try. You rock. Theo

NINE

The door opened a third time and Francesca was ready to tell them to go away. But it was her assistant, Joyce, who her brother insisted she hire. The younger girl stopped and stared around the room.

"Oh my god. Who barfed flowers and chocolate everywhere?" She glanced at Francesca at her desk. "I thought you were allergic to flowers."

Francesca sniffed. "I am."

"And I thought you didn't like chocolate," her assistant said.

"I don't."

The girl squealed and jumped around. "Then it's all for me?"

That made Francesca feel guilty as hell, but those were the facts. Goes to show one can't assume what a woman liked. Though, with these two guys, it was the thought that counted. And it did. Point for each. She wondered if she needed to start a score card. God, that sounded horrible. "Yup, all for you," Francesca said.

"Where did this come from?" Joyce asked.

"I went to a cocktail reception last night—"

Joyce looked at her. "You went to a party?"

"Yes," Francesca huffed. "What's wrong with that?"

"Nothing." Joyce seemed to backpedal. "But you're not the party type. Even though you're only a few years older than me, you're a lot older, if you get what I mean."

No. Francesca didn't get what she meant. "I go to parties," she said.

Joyce put hands on her hips. "Are you planning on coming to the party Shane is having tonight at the Prime house?"

Actually, she'd forgotten about that because she had no intention of going. "Yes," she said, "of course I'm going."

Joyce narrowed her eyes. The girl knew Francesca just made that up because of the accusation. Shit, did that mean she had to go now? *Stupid me.* Was she really so fuddy-duddy? Well, this should rock the girl's socks. "At the party last night, not only did I meet one guy, I met two. What do you think of that?"

The girl sucked in a breath. "OMG!" She hurried forward, dragging a chair behind her to the desk and plopped down. "You're a ménage?" she whispered loudly.

"A what?" Francesca was shocked by the word she heard from her assistant's mouth. "Ménage? No way! That's...that's..." she wasn't sure what it was, but it wasn't normal.

Joyce giggled. "There's nothing wrong with that, Francesca. Some shifters are meant for that. I hope I am. I mean, can you imagine, not one, but two gorgeous guys falling all over you to make sure you're happy and loved all the time? When one is making love to you, the other is cleaning the kitchen. Better yet, both making hot, sticky, love to you. It's nonstop orgasms for hours." Her entire body shook while Francesca's about came on the spot.

"That's quite a sexual fantasy there, Joyce. But that's not happening. My mom and dad were perfectly happy with just the two of them and that's how I'll be. I just need to figure out which I want and let the other go." That didn't feel as easy as it sounded.

"If that's what you feel, then that's perfect. Just saying that keeping both is a natural thing, too." She scooped up a chocolate shaped stapler on the desk and took a bite. "Yes, solid chocolate. Glad I didn't eat breakfast this morning." She stood from the chair. "If you don't pick the one who sent the liquid gold, send him my way. I'll take him any day."

The front door opened and her brother walked in. About time. He was getting in later and later. He eyed Joyce as she plopped onto the chair in front of Francesca's desk and grinned. A grin Francesca didn't like. The younger girl stiffened, her body freezing still. *That was odd*, Francesca thought.

"Good morning, Joyce, Francesca. Lovely seeing you both this morning." He came around to stand behind the assistant in the chair. He rested a hand on her shoulder. "You're coming to the party tonight, aren't you, Joyce?" She nodded.

"I am, too," Francesca said.

Her brother frowned. "Since when do you go to parties?"

God, she must be really pathetic. No wonder no one in the pride ever asked her out. "I go when I want. I haven't wanted to before. Besides, it's been a while since I've been to the house. I love my own little place, but it's nice to have luxury occasionally. I love the sofas in the living room. They're so cushy and great to relax on."

"I'll buy you one for your cottage," he said. She would've thanked him for the loving gesture if he'd expressed it with love, not disdain. Did he want her, his sister, not to go to a party at the prime house where he lived alone while their dad was at the nursing home getting better? That was ridiculous. He loved her, even though a tough guy like him never said those kind of things.

Francesca turned in her chair toward the side extension of her desk and stacked the checks entered into the accounting system. "These are ready for deposit. Everything is ready for month end closing." She swiveled back, holding up the paper-clipped bundle, to see Shane's hand had slid down the girl's arm and his finger was rubbing the underside of her breast.

He took the checks from her hand and headed down the hall toward his office. Francesca was shocked into silence. She'd never seen her brother make such a bold move in public. Were Shane and her assistant dating? By the ashamed expression on Joyce's face, she'd say no.

From down the hall, Shane called, "Joyce, bring me a cup of coffee to my office."

Francesca's eyes remained fixed on Joyce's downturned face. When the girl moved to get up, Francesca reached out and grabbed her arm. "Was that unwelcomed?" she asked. Then she thought unwelcomed or not, the office was not a place for shows of intimacy. Joyce shrugged.

"He likes me, I guess. I'm...flattered." She pulled away from Francesca's grip, headed toward the coffeemaker. The phone rang and a couple guys from the landscaping crew walked in. Friday at the office kicked into high gear and the incident slipped from Francesca's mind.

TEN

Why, oh why, did she say she was going to the prime house party? She must've not been thinking straight. Someone had accused her of being older than she was; that's what started this whole business.

She sat on the living room sofa she'd loved the day her mom picked it out and had it delivered. Dad complained because it was a bit expensive, but it wasn't like the pride was destitute. In fact, quite the opposite.

For many years, since the time of her grandfather, the pride had produced the best beef this side of the Mississippi. It started when her grandparents and a group of fellow tiger shifters settled here to escape persecution from humans. Good meat in large quantities was hard to find. So they purchased cows and bulls and set to cultivating what they considered good eatin'.

Seemed others thought so, too. As money came in, the pride purchased more land and bred more cattle. They were able to acquire quite a bit of forested area and grazing pasture for both building homes and feeding herds. The pride was still small compared to other shifter communities that had been around for a while. But they had the money to sustain a level of comfort few others could afford.

Her parents knew the meaning of hard work since they were part of the generation who worked day and night to establish what they had today. That trait seemed to be lost more and more with each new generation born with everything they wanted and needed in life.

She and her brother knew the meaning of work, but not necessarily hard work. Since their teens, they spent time after school working in the office or doing chores. Francesca considered it work because they couldn't sit around and play games or watch TV mindlessly.

And based on stories from her grandfather and father working the cattle and doing heavy physical labor, office work wasn't physically demanding. Though today with the flowers and chocolate consuming her office, it might have been considered physically demanding.

With her last sneeze being hours ago, she relaxed and munched on snacks Shane had set out for guests to eat. He'd just turned the music up to the point it was annoying. The original prime house had been deemed to small and antiquated about ten years ago.

So this new "cabin," straight out of a luxury travel and leisure magazine, had speakers throughout the house and outside, a large pool, wired for Wi-Fi, professional kitchen appliances, a bathroom for every bedroom, and TVs in almost every room hooked up to satellite service.

Her little cottage was definitely a step, or leap, down, but it was hers.

Several other ladies and some guys gathered in the living room with her. She knew everyone as all knew her as the prime's daughter. She tried to be nice and outgoing with others, even though she wasn't the party-goer type. And she was reminded why when the next song thumped with her building headache.

Much of the pride had shown. The parents and older generations were just about gone for the night. They drank wine or beer, chatted while chasing around the young ones or making sure none of the grandkids drowned in the pool. Now, it was bedtime for both age groups.

With the departure came the younger ones, the music being cranked, and hard liquor made a bigger appearance. No more splashing in the pool, but the hot tub was filled with semi-naked people doing who knows what with hands under the bubbling water.

Her brother walked through the large open space separating the interior from the outside. Their parents had installed one of those glass folding doors that slid to the sides and practically disappeared so you couldn't tell where the house stopped and patio began.

Shane had his arm wrapped around a young twenty-something, which she thought was age inappropriate to his young thirty-something.

The girl was younger than Joyce. Hold on a second. He wasn't dating Joyce? Then what the hell was the boob massage he gave her assistant this morning?

Francesca was about to confront her brother when she saw the females around her eyeing the couple. Some gave the girl a vicious stink eye, while others looked worried. What was going on? Time to find out.

Francesca set her glass of water on the table and approached Shane and the girl, Mirla, if Francesca remembered correctly. She stopped in front of them, earning a scowl from her brother. "Hi, Mirla," she yelled over the music. "Can I talk to Shane for a minute?"

Mirla turned her ear toward Francesca. "What?"

"I said," she repeated, "I'd like to talk to my brother."

The girls smiled and hollered, "Yeah, this is your brother."

Francesca wanted to bang her head on the wall. This wasn't going like she hoped. Instead of using words, Francesca pointed at Mirla, then pointed to the empty chair Francesca just abandoned. The teeny-bopper smile faded and the chick shook her head. Obviously, she got the meaning, but didn't respond correctly.

Francesca gave her the "mad mom" look: one brow raised, the other eye squinted almost shut, lips pressed into a thin line, nostrils flaring. The female paled and nearly jumped onto the cushioned chair. Huh, maybe she would make a good mom someday.

Shane grabbed his sister's arm and dragged her down the hallway to a quieter place. "What the hell are you doing, Francesca?"

"I could ask you the same damn question," she replied. Her fisted hands landed on her hips. "I thought you liked Joyce."

Shane stepped back. "Joyce who?"

Francesca's jaw dropped. "The Joyce you fondled in the office this morning."

His pissed-off expression turned conciliatory. "Oh, that." He brushed it off with a wave. "That was an accident." *Right,* Francesca thought. "That girl is too young for me." He tried to push past her, but Francesca wasn't done yet.

"Too young? How old is the one you just had under your arm?"

His pacified semblance turned angry again. "Look, Francesca. Who I date is none of your business. Just like I don't bother you about who you date."

Now that she thought about it, he didn't ask anything about the flowers in the office. Maybe he was respecting boundaries and she wasn't. "You'd better tell Joyce then so you're not leading her on. And keep your hands off her. The office is no place for public displays of affection."

He raised both hands in supplication. "You're right. I apologize. Can we get back to the party now?" She turned. "Francesca, wait." She looked over her shoulder at him. "Thanks for coming. You never show up. I didn't think you were the party type."

"I'm not." She turned and sighed. "I'm here to prove to myself that I'm not ready for the house full of cats and the old lady name that goes with it."

Shane wrapped an arm around her shoulder and walked her through the hall. "I'm proud of you, little sis. Let's get you a drink."

"My water's on the coffee table in the living room."

"No. I mean a real drink. A grownup girl deserves a grownup drink, don't you think?"

She snorted. "No. But I've always wanted one of those beverages with a tiny umbrella that you see on commercials with people at beaches on vacation."

They reached the end of the hall where the music roared. "All right, little sis. One Sex on the Beach coming up." He slapped her ass and headed for the bar. What the hell did she just order?

ELEVEN

The party at the prime house rolled into the night. And this the most sex on the beach Francesca had ever had—the drink that is. The shit was so sweet, it was like drinking juice for breakfast, with a little zinger. And the saying that shifters couldn't get drunk—that wasn't really the case.

Shifter metabolism was so much faster than humans' that when drinking at the same speed, shifters burned off the alcohol much faster than their counterparts. But there's a limit to everything.

If shifters drank enough, quick enough— enough that would kill a human—they could get drunk. But it was short lived when the drinking stopped, like fewer than twenty minutes.

She'd never giggled so much in her life. Actually, she thought all her brother's friends were lame and show-offish. Now she added dork to that list of adjectives. One of said friends laid an arm across her shoulders.

"Hey there, short stuff," he said, "how's it going down there." She looked up at him. Jim, the independent accountant they worked with. He had always been too cute for his own good. And too tall.

"Not bad. How is it above the clouds tonight?" she asked. Jim looked away and nodded at someone. She followed his line of sight to see her brother smiling at him.

"Not bad, either." He grabbed her around the waist and lifted her over his head like she weighed nothing. "Let me show you!" She squealed and he took off running down one of the paths leading off the patio into the forest.

The little light from the twinklies draped in the trees at the house quickly faded to black. Fortunately, her animal saw perfectly in the dark. She laughed harder when Jim started making caveman grunts and bouncing her into the air. Then her stomach lurched. So not good.

"Jim," she shouted, "put me down before I puke." She was on her feet so quickly, her head spun, which didn't help her stomach. She leaned to the side to get her balance and he caught her up against a tree.

"You okay?" he asked. "I didn't mean to upset your stomach."

"I'm fine. Just need to stop moving in ways we're not meant to," she said.

Jim looked around and down at his watch. "Francesca, since you're here, I got a question to ask you."

This sounded almost serious. "Sure, ask away."

"I got this friend who likes this girl and he doesn't know how to ask her out."

Was he serious? This guy was almost thirty years old, as were his friends. Not only should he know how to ask a girl out, he and his friends should be mated and thinking about kids. But she wasn't much younger and she hadn't thought much about it until last night.

Francesca didn't know what to say really. Treat the girl like a lady and respect her wishes and give her all the love and sex she wanted. Sounded reasonable to her.

Jim kept asking lame questions and glancing at his watch. She felt like she was taking a timed test where she had only so long to spit out the answers. Just abruptly as his first question, Jim said he knew what to tell his friend.

"I'll walk you back to the house," he said.

"Thanks," she replied, "but I'll hang around here for a while. It's been a long time since I was in these woods. Used to play here a lot." He said bye and hurried off. The man was stranger than she thought. But he seemed nice and he did their taxes and banking stuff, which she didn't want to do with everything else she had on her plate.

She loved the peaceful solitude of nature, even though the outdoors didn't love her too much. As long as she had her allergy medicine, all was fine. Sort of. It was getting late and she'd had enough of parties with the past two nights.

The closer to the house she got, the louder the music. Someone needed to turn it down, seriously. If there were any neighbors within a half-mile radius, they would've called the cops by now. The only reason she heard the whimper was because the music was between songs.

She stopped walking to listen. The sound came from the sitting area where she used to watch hummingbirds sip at the bird feeders. She went in search of the quiet cry. Closer to the area, she heard it again. This time mumbled words made it to her ears, but the music had returned, blocking out most of it.

Her step quickened, hands batting away limbs as her eyes recognized the obstructions. She burst into the small clearing to see a couple guys her brother's age standing around, deeply entranced by something happening in the center of the cove.

Francesca shoved past the men to see a female held face down over a small table, her skirt pushed up around her waist. A second man was unbuckling his pants.

The guy forcing the woman to lie on the table spoke. "Hurry up, man. I want to fuck her before the alcohol wears off. I've wanted to do this bitch since she turned me down. I'll show her who gets the last fuck."

The hate in his voice was so harsh, it froze Francesca in her place.

"It's not supposed to be like that," another said. "We're growing the pride—"

"I don't give a fuck what—" The pissed-off guy looked over his shoulder at the men and saw Francesca momentarily in shock.

The man she recognized as a relative newcomer, Nielson something, released his hold on the female and came toward her. "Well, look here. The prima bitch wants fucked, too. You definitely need it, you're so—" The man didn't finish as Francesca lifted her knee to the side, pivoted, and delivered a kick to his chest, sending him ass over head into a tree.

The man who'd dropped his pants next to the woman fell over backward, trying to scramble away and jerk his pants up at the same time. Behind her, she heard leaves crunch under a footfall coming closer. The attacker was too close to pop a kick, so she stepped forward, spun around, and slammed a punch to his solar plexus with the heel of her hand. He dropped like a rag doll.

She glared at the other man standing around. "Anyone else want to try?" Within a blink, he'd disappeared into the trees. Francesca scooped the female off the table, straightened her skirt, and set her on a bench. The girl was a neighbor of her parents, in her senior year of high school. A baby.

Fury swirled in Francesca's heart and soul. The men she'd taken down were gone. If she'd vented on them, they would be dead. Instead, she gathered little Luci into her arms and stomped off for the house. So much shit was going to hit the fan, it wasn't funny.

Francesca placed the girl in the guest bathroom in the house. "Lock this door, and don't let anyone in but me. Understand?"

She had to verify the girl heard her because the music was so fucking loud. Which was another thing she'd take care of.

Francesca caught Nielsen limping toward the front of the house. "You!" she yelled. "I'm not through with you, you son of a bitch." She dropped kicked him into the cabin's side. He hit and slid down. He started a shift, but she wrestled him into a choke hold and dragged him around back and tossed him into the pool.

She ran through the patio and first floor, turning lights on and slapping drinks from hands. When she reached the sound system, she punched the power button with her finger and ripped off the volume control. The sudden silence threw her off balance for a second.

Sounds of groans and voiced complaints peppered the air. She turned and shouted get out. As if coming from a daze, others looked around wondering what was going on. Some fixing eyes on her. She was sure she was a sight to see. But no one was moving fast enough.

Her feline said she'd take care of that. Bone snapped and tendons stretched as Francesca's cat came to the surface. She took a deep breath and roared with the prima power she was born with.

That did it.

An eruption of mass proportion of bodies flying into the forest and out the front door satisfied her. Only one came at her. Shane.

"What the fuck are you doing? This is my party." He was so angry, he'd started a partial shift also. But she had a head start on him. She loved her brother, but what she'd just experienced with Nielson and Luci set her on the edge.

Her body transformed further, ripping her dress, and she lunged at Shane, taking him down and rolling them both across the patio. Her martial arts practice came in handy. She easily pinned him on his stomach and shifted enough to speak.

"Then control your fucking guests, or I will make sure there are no more parties." She pushed off him, back to her full human form, and headed toward where she left Luci in the bathroom.

TWELVE

Francesca lay on the sofa in her cottage listening to the birds chirp in the late-morning sun. She thought back to how Luci had begged her not to tell her parents what happened. At first, Francesca flat-out told her no. Her parents needed to know exactly what happened.

After thirty minutes of tears and a near anxiety breakdown on the girl's part, Francesca relented on the condition that she and her friends at the party be at Francesca's house at 11 a.m. sharp. They were also to bring any other females they knew from the party. She didn't expect many since it was such short notice and she was right.

At 11 a.m., her doorbell rang. Luci and two others her age stood contrite at her screen door. "Come in," she said. The girls followed her to the kitchen where Francesca had hot waffles and sausage waiting in covered dishes. "Have you eaten breakfast yet?" The girls shook their heads.

Francesca motioned for them to sit while she pulled plates and forks. If these girls were like she was in her teen years, sleep was far more important than eating breakfast and getting up early, before noon, on a weekend was a killer.

As they ate, Francesca asked about school, and they talked and laughed about teachers they shared and ragged on the ones everyone disliked for one reason or another. Not much had changed since her time there—only the kids themselves change as each year graduates a group and brings in a new.

After the table was cleared and the girls helped to wash and put away dishes, they sat in the living room. The air became awkward, but Francesca expected that. What she was wanting to talk about was awkward. She'd never experienced such violence before and didn't know how to approach it. But it had to be talked about. She couldn't let this go.

"All right, young lady," Francesca said, "tell me how you let yourself get in such a situation. You have to know better." The girl stared down at her hands in her lap. "Luci, what can you tell me? Do the others know what went on?" She referred to the friends beside the girl.

Luci said, "I don't remember much. Just you telling me to lock the bathroom door then I threw up in the toilet. Later you dropped me at my house."

"What do you girls think happened?" Francesca asked them.

They shrugged, still not saying anything. How was she going to get through to three seniors in high school who thought they were invincible and life was always going to be as good as it was in their parents' home where they had everything their hearts desired, including safety?

"Okay, since you don't want to share, I'll start. I will layout a scenario, granted a worst case, but very likely based on what I've seen in the world. Are you all willing to picture this in your minds as I tell it?" Again, they quietly nodded.

"Good. Let's say I wasn't at the party to stop those men from what they were about to do." Francesca quickly put together a scene that would break her heart when she saw it, which unfortunately was too often in the world.

"Luci, you work ten-hour days cleaning houses for minimum wage which puts you at poverty level. You share a roach-infested room in a condemned shack which means half the time you and your baby sleep on the floor while your roommate takes the bed.

"You didn't finish school because the sneers and bullying about being pregnant became too much, not to mention your parents were so ashamed, they didn't want you living in the house to make a bad example for your little sister.

"All the food you can afford consists of bouillon cubes you dissolve in water. You tear mold off the hamburger buns you found in the trash behind a burger shop and soak that in the broth. You hope it keeps the baby's stomach from growling, because you became too thin for your body to continue producing breast milk."

"Stop," Luci said with tears on her cheeks. "I've heard enough." She looked at her friends then her hands again. "We'd heard things from other girls about how some of the guys were looking at some of the younger ones. Like us. No one ever pays us any attention. When guys like them, like girls like us, it's special. It makes me feel good inside. Like I'm important." She wiped a tear. "I didn't think they'd get so...pushy and spouting things like how it's the guys' responsibility to bring honor and power to the pride. The males protected the females and the females..."

"The females what?" Francesca asked.

She shrugged. "I don't know."

Francesca sighed. "I'm sure I don't have to mention how underage drinking played you right into their hands, do I, Luci?" The girl shook her head. "Here's the rule you three are going to follow until each of you have a mate."

They looked at her like she was crazy.

She laughed. "I know that seems forever away, but time disappears the older you get. You'll see. Anyway, the rule: Never, ever, leave one of you alone except to go into the bathroom stall. Got it?" They smiled.

"I mean it. We girls have to watch out for each other. Especially when there are others around we don't know. Do any of you know this Nielson guy?" They shook their heads. "Didn't think so. He's new around here. Been here a few months now.

"Think of it this way, even though it sounds harsh: if something bad happens to one of you because you weren't together, you are all responsible because you now know to always be together."

"Like Juliette," Mirla said.

"What happened to Juliette?" she asked. Francesca knew the girl transferred to a different high school not too long ago, but didn't know why. Last time Francesca saw her was at a get-together at the prime house a while back.

"She's pregnant," Luci whispered. Francesca about choked. Now she felt bad about the example story she made up earlier. It must've hit closer to home than she intended for the girls.

"Is the father her mate, even though she's so young?" Francesca asked, hoping they could be high school sweethearts or something as nice.

Luci shook her head. "She doesn't know who the father is. She said she never had sex."

Francesca sat back in the seat. That shouldn't be possible. She was speechless. The girl had to be protecting the male's identity. She hoped the couple loved each other and the child would have a good life.

"I'm sorry, Miss Virgata, for not being more vigilant," Luci continued. "It was the prime's house. I knew you wouldn't let anything bad happen. We won't let it happen again." All the girls agreed.

Francesca definitely had to talk with Shane. This would never happen again. Times like this she really wished her mother was still alive. She didn't know what to ask or what to do. She had no experience with this kind of thing. Neither of the guys had actually done anything to Luci.

Could she press charges even if the victim didn't remember anything and nothing happened? This was so frustrating for her. Maybe Marcus could help. He was so intelligent. She glanced at the clock.

In the text she received from Marcus last night, he said he'd be by around 4:00 p.m. to pick her up for an early dinner before the show. He didn't give any hints to where they were going except the words "a lion among ladies is a most dreadful thing." She had no clue what that meant. As far as she knew, there were no lions in the pride. Only tigers. Theo was a lion, but as far as she knew, Theo and Marcus didn't know each other.

"Okay, here's what we're going to do," Francesca said. "Luci, keep your distance from the new guy, Nielson. Don't let him near you, don't go into a room or vehicle with him. He really doesn't like you for some reason." The girl blushed, "I mean it, Luci. He wanted to hurt you."

The teen looked up with fear in her eyes. Good, she understood the seriousness of the situation. Francesca continued. "I want you girls to be extra vigilant when older guys are around. Don't let them bully you into something you don't want to do. Remember my story about getting pregnant. None of you are ready to start a family. Finish school first. Got it?"

They nodded. "Yes, Miss Virgata," each said. Nothing else came to mind so she walked them to the door and told them to be careful driving home.

God, she hoped she did the right thing.

THIRTEEN

Marcus had to rope down his bear to keep it from jumping on their mate the second they saw her. She wore a sexy, flowy skirt with a top that hugged those delicious curves. When she answered the front door after he rang the bell, they almost didn't make it to the show because he wanted to haul her into her bedroom and show her how much she affected him.

Instead, he smiled and straightened his tie, "Ready?" Then she looked at him and his body tingled, his heart raced. How was he so lucky to have found his mate?

"Yup." She locked the house and he escorted her to the passenger side of his Accord. One thing about being an accountant was you'd never become a millionaire. Only those with the letters CEO after their name received that privilege. But that's not why he did what he did.

The drive over was quiet but comfortable. He'd never been to this place and depended on Siri to get them there. After finding a parking spot in the crowded lot, he let out a breath and relaxed. He wondered if he held his breath the entire drive.

Damn, he was pathetic around his mate. He really needed to socialize more to get into the habit of talking again. Sitting all day in front of a computer killed that urge to communicate. Except when he got frustrated and yelled at the damn thing, threatening to throw it out the window.

Francesca looked around the grassy area that sloped steeply to an outdoor amphitheater. "Are we watching a play? Outside?"

"Yeah," he said, "it's 'Shakespeare in the Park.' Actors come from all over to perform Shakespeare's many plays. We're seeing *A Midsummer's Night Dream.*"

"I've heard of that one, but never read it," Francesca replied.

"Good, then you'll be entertained," he said. "It's a comedy about the events surrounding the marriage of the Duke of Athens, Theseus, and Hippolyta."

"Oh," was all she said. He knew she'd love it. Mates were always compatible.

He opened her door and offered a hand. Like velvet, her hand slid into his. They fit perfectly together. He popped the trunk with the key fob and took out a blanket, grocery bag stuffed with food, and a huge bean bag.

When sitting on the ground, one had to prepare to be comfortable. Hard dirt did not conform to the ass, but a bean bag did. Unfortunately, it was Theo's, which the doofus used when he played video games. So the bag was bright yellow with Hulk Hogan and other WWF wrestlers on it. He'd just throw a blanket over it and no one would know the difference.

After finding an open spot on the steep grassy incline, he helped Francesca sit then proceeded to unload the paper bag. He had no idea what she liked, so he bought the shifter basics: T-bone steak bites, filet mignon bites, stuffed bacon wraps, wienies on a stick, and chicken wings.

"Wow, Marcus," she said. "You didn't have to go through so much trouble for me." She took a bacon wrap and bit off half. "Mmm. I'm glad you did, though. These are great." Pride soared through him and his bear. They showed their mate they could feed her.

Nestled into the bean bag with food

surrounding them, Francesca asked what he did for a living.

"I'm a forensic accountant," he said.

Francesca raised a brow. "It sounds half fun, half boring."

He laughed. "Often times, it's both. It's like finding a needle in a haystack. There are hundreds or thousands of transactions and I have to find the few that show the crime whether that's laundering, embezzlement, fraud of any kind."

"Sounds difficult. Where does the fun part come in?" she asked.

"That comes after finding the evidence that will put the criminal away for years. Some of these guys steal from employees' retirement funds. They ensure their own future with yachts and fancy cars while the people have to work up to the day they die because the money they saved is gone. I work for ones who can't speak up for themselves because of a legitimate fear like losing their job."

Francesca turned to look at him, like really look at him. "You actually care for others, don't you? You've devoted your life to helping those being taken advantage of. I'm impressed, Marcus. Guys like you are few and far between."

He felt his face heat to the temperature of

the sun. "Enough about me," he said. "Tell me about you."

"Me?" Why did his interest in her surprise her? She was the sexiest, most beautiful women he'd ever met. "I'm quite boring full-time. I sit in the office all day doing office stuff."

"Thursday at the meet and greet you mentioned you worked at your pride's place of business," he said. "You take care of them?"

"Yeah, that's the office requirement. Folks are in and out all day. Some just to say hello. But since Dad's been sick, we get fewer of the older ones coming in."

"Does your brother work there, too?" he asked.

"It's a family thing. When Mom was alive, we all worked there; Shane and me after school. Now he comes in whenever and I send him out to run errands. Deposit checks, pull out petty cash, purchase supplies. Things like that." She smirked. "And he's friends with our tax professional, so he's there a lot, too, it seems."

"Oh, yes," she said, "I got your..." she paused, seemingly thinking about something, "delivery at the office yesterday. Thank you so much."

"You're very welcome. I hope you like flowers."

Her smile melted him. "Well, I'm allergic to pollen, so I stick with plants."

He pulled away from her but placed a hand on her shoulder. "I am so sorry. I had no idea you were allergic."

"No problem," she said. "Of course you didn't know. But I have to say the office was stunning all decorated and smelled great. When I wasn't sneezing." Her smile softened her words that he took as teasing. "Are you working on a forensics case now?"

"I am. I don't want to bore you with the details, but this case will send someone to prison for a long time."

She gasped. "No, please. Bore me with the details. Is it a huge banking scandal or something?"

She was so cute when excited. "Nah, nothing that grandiose. A wealthy corporation head is stealing money from the company in large amounts. The guy must be an idiot. The business's 1120s and backup data aren't even close to reconciling.

"What's so bad about this guy is that he's linked to a scam artist who's on the FBI's wanted list. The scammer targets others like a crooked televangelist. Hollowman is his name; he tells people what they want to hear, makes false promises, and demands money from them. More and more until the unsuspecting person is in bankruptcy. The man has been doing this for years."

"He's not been caught?" she asked.

"No. He's very slick. He can spot easy prey in a heartbeat. Take almost any situation and turn it to his advantage. He craves money and power over people. He's sadistic. Then somehow he knows when to get out, which is usually right before we get to him. I've actually worked several cases that involved him. We'll get him eventually. The good guy always wins in the end."

"Wow," Francesca said. "It's hard to comprehend how the scammer gets into others' heads and almost brainwashes them. I saw a show on the History Channel about a fake preacher who finagled an entire town of its money. It was heartbreaking."

He ran a fingertip along the top of her hand. He said, "It's good to know you care about others, too. I deal with the ugly side of humanity most of the time. It's nice to have someone like you around to remind me not everyone is out for themselves."

Her cheeks blushed. So pretty. She shrugged. "That's how I was raised—to love others and give the benefit of the doubt."

"As beautiful inside and out. I'm one lucky guy." He lifted her hand to his lips and kissed it.

FOURTEEN

Theo hummed to himself as he searched a bathroom drawer for a band to hold his hair back. He didn't want it blocking his sight to his mate. It's been so long since he'd seen her, his lion almost busted out to go in search of her scent. She was a tiger and he knew of only one tiger group that would be close enough to come to that party last Thursday night.

Just thinking back to her smell, her eyes, her to-die-for body, made him as hard as the granite of his bathroom counter. Damn, maybe he should take care of that before he left to get her. Didn't want that popping up at an inopportune time—like every time he looked at her.

He'd texted her earlier to dress casual. No

dress or heels. This would be a relaxed, fun day. He would dress up for her, though. A clean T-shirt and jeans with no big holes showing off his men's bikini undies.

Red with black tiger stripes today. Then again, maybe she'd like to see that he thought about her when choosing his underwear for the day. Was that too pervy on a first date?

He slammed the drawer closed, disgusted that he couldn't find a clip. Maybe he could borrow one of hers. Then he'd keep it and be able to smell her all night while he worked and slept and have great sex dreams. Maybe that was a bit too pervy, too. Then again, they were all adults, right?

Most of us, his lion said.

Theo slipped the tickets and his phone in one back jean pocket and his wallet in the other, then strolled into the kitchen for a bite before he left. His roomie sat reading the Sunday paper with a cup of coffee at his side.

"So," Marcus said, "you're really taking her to this thing? Aren't you worried she'll think you're crazy?"

"Dude," Theo replied, "this is a hundred times more exciting than anything Shakespeare wrote. 'Romeo, Romeo, where the hell art thou?'" He pulled a bag of granola from the cabinet. "Are you sure she stayed awake for the whole thing?"

"Oh, I'm sure she was awake for the whole play. I never took my eyes from her." Marcus eyed him for his reaction. Bastard. He wasn't about to give the dick any satisfaction. Then he remembered about giving his own dick satisfaction before leaving. He'd skip that. He should leave soon.

"Whatever. We're letting her decide, right?" he said.

Marcus agreed. "That we are. Have a great time. Make sure she calls me if she needs rescued."

Theo snorted. "Yeah, you're funny, Mr. Sit On My Ass All Day."

"You're just jealous because I use my brain to work and you have to hoof it."

"Again, I say, whatever. I'm much more fun than you are. You can't deny it," Theo said.

"But Francesca isn't the wild and crazy dork you are," he countered.

"We'll see, won't we." Theo smiled, waved goodbye with his middle finger and walked out the door after grabbing two helmets.

Outside her cute little home, Theo stared

at her gorgeous body in tight jeans, form fitting top, and slip-on flats. Damn, she was smokin'. She was also staring with her mouth open.

"So," he said, "guess you've never ridden on a motorcycle before?"

Her head rotated side to side and her eyes roamed from one end of the bike to the other. "I don't think I'll fit."

His face broke into a grin, keeping back the nasty thoughts racing through his mind. Oh yeah, baby. It'll fit just right, nice and tight. He put down the kickstand and grab the helmet he brought for her. Strolling up to her on the porch, he felt her eyes burn a line up and down his body. He knew he had an effect on women, didn't know what it was about him, but he never cared until now.

This was the only woman he'd ever want again. The only woman who mattered in his life. He would do whatever it took to make her happy with everything about him. He wanted her to choose him. His lion and he knew she was their mate. They would be devastated if she walked away.

He slid the helmet on her head and flipped up the visor. "Safety first, my love. I always want you safely by my side." Her eyes and nostrils flared a second before returning to normal. He took her hand and guided her to the bike. Then he noticed how short she was. How did he not notice that before? Her size didn't matter. Just his.

"Okay," he said, "here's what we're goin' to do." He turned to her. "I'm going to squat and you get on my back."

"What?" With the helmet on, it came out more like, "Wa?"

"You know, like piggyback riding." He crouched. She backed away.

"Oh, no way. I'll break you. Look at me," she said.

He looked over his shoulder at her. "Gladly, baby." His eyes roamed over every luscious curve. Her face blushed red. "Now get over here and put your arms around my neck so I can lift you onto the bike with me." Hurry up before I come from staring and fantasizing.

She let out a big sigh and walked up to him and tentatively leaned against him. He barely held back the groan/growl from her breasts pressed onto his back. Her arms wrapped around his neck and her sweet smell surrounded him. Fuck. He wanted to roll her to the ground and drive into her waiting heat. Shit, he hoped she didn't smell how desperate he was to have her. He could potentially make a very big ass of himself—to Marcus's delight, no doubt.

His hands then slid down the back of her thighs to the back of her knees. He felt a shudder go through her. Well, damn. Something popped up on him already. He should've taken care of that at home. Not much he could do about it now.

With powerful legs, he stretched to stand, pulling her body against his. The heat from her pussy on his back almost took him to the ground. Fuck. He smelled her want—as strong as his. Was it tacky to ask your mate to mate before the first date even started?

No. He would not do that. He would court her like she deserved. At least once. Not sure about waiting the second time, though.

At that moment, he realized that if he tried to straddle his bike seat with the hard-on he had, he'd have a new hole in his jeans where he'd rather not have one. Now what? He'd have to do what he normally did in this situation, walk it off.

He bounced her higher onto his back, getting a squeal from her, and headed around the backside of her home.

"What are you doing?" she hollered. "The motorcycle's that way."

"I know, babe. I just need to take care of an inflamed muscle before we get going," he responded, hopefully cryptically.

"What? I can't hear you very well with this helmet smashing my ears. Did you strain your back or ankle? See, I told you I was too heavy," she returned.

"I'll show you heavy," he said. With another bounce up his back, he bolted for the woods. Her full torso rubbed against his back, from lush tits to wet pussy. Oh fuck, she was wet now. Not helping his dick relax any.

Her laughter sang in his ears. His spirits burst with happiness after not seeing her for so long. This was the first time he'd really been happy since losing his family as a child. He would do whatever it took to keep her safe and by his side.

Coming around the side of thick brush, Theo came to an abrupt stop, seeing a guy about his age balls deep in a female bent forward against a tree. Fortunately, Francesca was sitting too low on his back to see over his shoulder and the helmet blocked the little sound. The guy met his eyes with a flash of gold. The man's animal glaring? His nose told him tiger, alpha. Francesca's brother? Doing some chick in the woods?

Francesca bounced on his back. "Why did you stop? I can't see around you."

The man's eyes narrowed. He must've heard his sister's voice. The female the alpha had his dick in mumbled. The brother reached forward and slapped her face. Talk about awkward. Theo quickly stepped backward to the other side of the brush and made a quick jog back to the cottage and bike.

"Sorry, babe. The muscle finally relaxed," like completely after that visual, "time to get back to the bike. We got a show to go crazy at."

"What kind of show?" she asked.

He grinned even though she couldn't see it. "Just you wait, darlin'. You're gonna love it."

FIFTEEN

Her hands clamped over her ears, Francesca stood in the first row of the arena and screamed as loud as her throat would let her, yet those next to her still couldn't hear her. The monster truck U Ain't Lion soared over the row of smashed cars and bounced to a victory at the far end. She threw her hands into the air and jumped up and down and hugged Theo screaming beside her.

When the trucks punched the gas pedal to race toward the ramp, she'd never heard anything so loud in her life. Decibels reached 110. Brains oozed out ears at around 125 decibels. Damn, she loved this. She yelled and whistled as the truck made its lap around the ring before exiting.

Theo turned to her and yelled right in her ear, but it was just a muddle of sound. She shrugged and he grabbed her hand, leading her to the side where there was an entrance onto the arena floor.

The guard stopped them, but Theo kept his eyes on the truck. When it got to where they stood, the driver saw Theo and waved him in. The guard opened the gate and Theo dragged her out the entrance to where the trucks were staged until their turn to jump.

They headed back to the pit and there in all its glory stood U Ain't Lion. The front engine compartment was painted like the open mouth of a lion, razor teeth most prominent. The body was a saddle gold color with fur accents added in.

Two huge eyeballs that glowed encompassed the windshield. And the best part was the massive mane that surrounded the cab and doors of the truck. When the truck raced forward, it blew in the wind. Looked kick-ass from the stands.

Theo ran up to the lion truck and guy-hugged the driver when he was on the ground. Their mouths moved, but she heard basically nothing. And probably wouldn't until next week sometime. Her tigress disappeared a long time ago when the first truck blasted through the banner covering the entrance, setting off the fireworks.

Her date waved her over and put an arm around her and squeezed her to his side. "Francesca, this is my cousin, Simba."

The man reached out and shook her hand. "Simba is my stage name. You can call me Bob." A burst of laughter escaped her at the dichotomy of the two names. "Did y'all like that jump? That was the most air I'd caught in a while."

Theo kissed Francesca's temple. "My lady here is pure luck."

"And you're damn lucky, cuz," Bob said. "They need to check out the truck before the next run. Come on to the tent. I'll show you around."

Francesca felt in a surreal world. Like that part of Alice in Wonderland where she's really tiny and everything around her is gigantic in size. She was half the height of the tires on most the trucks. While Bob rushed around doing his things, Theo wrapped himself around her from behind and snuggled her to him. He felt so good, and smelled divine. Totally different from Marcus, but just as good.

Her mind wandered toward her date with Marcus last night. It was incredible. He was perfect, the food and play were icing on the filet mignon. And his kiss when he dropped her off...her toes curled in her shoes.

Theo leaned down to her ear, taking a deep breath. "I don't know what you're thinking, but I like it."

Guilt struck her heart. She tried to suppress it as much as she could so Theo wouldn't ask her about it. She'd hoped after these first dates with each, she'd know who she wanted more. But she wanted them the same. Choosing one over the other—the idea of losing either—sent her close to an anxiety attack.

God, she was so confused.

Theo took her hand. "Let's walk around and check things out." The weather was perfect. Sunshine and in the eighties with a light breeze. Days like this her animal wanted to roll onto her back and let it all hang out while she sunned her belly.

"What do think so far?" he asked.

She instantly smiled up at him. "This is great. I've never been to one of these before. Now, I'm a fan."

He squeezed her to his side. "Yeah, that's my girl. Let's get something to eat. You ever had fried Twinkies before?"

"There is such a thing?" she asked.

He stopped and turned her to him. "Woman, when was the last time you went to the fair or carnival or any of that?"

Her heart sank, even though it wasn't intentional on his part. The last county fair she and her family had attended was just before her mom passed away.

"Baby, what's wrong? I didn't mean to make you upset." His rough fingers brushed the side of her face, leaving chills in their stead.

"No, it's not your fault. It's just that my last time at the fair was before the cancer took my mom from us. That was a long time ago."

He gathered her to his chest in a hug. "Oh, baby. I'm sorry. I didn't mean to bring up sad memories."

She sighed, holding back surprising tears. "I'm good. It was a long time ago. Long enough that they didn't have fried Twinkies."

He stepped back to put her at arm's length. "Well, it's time you had one. Let's go." He grabbed her hand and ran across the pavement toward the vendors' area of the show. She laughed as he tried to get her to hurry along, but big girls like her didn't run anywhere. Her body was made for loving, not track and field.

A short time later, they sat at a picnic table under flashing lights with rock music blaring over speakers high on poles throughout the lot. Between them were an assortment of goodies: fried Twinkies, fried Oreos, a fried Snickers bar, funnel cake with extra powdered sugar, and two hot dogs Cincinnati style. She was going to be sick after this, but loving every bite on the way.

"You know," Theo said, "I lost my mom when I was young, too. Along with my dad and brother."

Francesca nearly choked on her Oreo. "Oh my god. What happened?"

"Mom and Dad had friends who rented a beach house for a week every summer and they invited us out. Those were great times. Neither Mom nor Dad did any work. They left laptops at home. They were there totally for my brother and me.

"At that time, a punk street gang of lions decided to have an initiation that included shooting out tires of cars on the road. We were coming back from the beach on the Interstate traveling sixty to sixty-five miles an hour.

"I don't remember the accident, don't remember the bullet shattering my dad's side window, don't remember the eighteen-wheeler we veered into the path of. I only remember the face of the fireman who looked through my window of our upside-down car and said he would get me out."

Francesca squeezed his hand, her heart

breaking for him. She wondered if his lion purposely took those frightening memories from him. Letting the child heal from something so tragic, it would break another person. "Is that why you became a fireman?"

He smiled at her. "It is. I wanted to do for someone else what that man did for me. He saved my life in more ways than one." He stared down at the nearly untouched sweets between them. "You eat the Snickers bar and I'll cut the Twinkie in half."

"Oh," she said, "I don't care much for chocolate. You can have that. I'll try the Oreos."

"Well, shit," he said.

"What?" She looked around for something wrong.

"I sent you all that chocolate the other day and you don't like the darn stuff."

That had completely slipped her mind. Joyce had taken it all, flowers and chocolate, home so the office would be aired out by Monday and no more sneezing. "I meant to thank you for it. I forgot totally about that. Thank you so much," she said.

"Yeah, but you don't like chocolate." He was cute with his scowl.

"But that's okay because my assistant who does love chocolate is now in love with you. In fact, she said to pass her number to you."

Theo came over the top of the table—over the top--and scooped her into his lap. He took her chin in his huge hands. "Listen up, baby girl. Know this right now, there is no one else for me, ever. You are her. The one I will always sleep next to at night and wake up to in the morning." He brought his lips to hers and took possession of her mouth, her tongue, her heart.

When he pulled away, she panted for air. He brushed hair from her face. "I know I'm being too forward for our first date, but the moment I laid eyes on you, my lion and I both knew you were what we've been waiting for."

Suddenly, the cryptic text message from Marcus made sense: a lion among ladies is a most dreadful thing. But there was no way Marcus could know she had a date with Theo. They couldn't possibly know each other, could they?

SIXTEEN

Dammit. Francesca hated being late for anything. Even though she was usually the only one in the office, besides Joyce, she still hated being late. After parking in her designated spot, her assistant came bouncing out the front door, all smiles. That wasn't normal.

"Thank you, thank you, thank you!" Joyce hugged her as soon as she stepped from the car.

"Why are you thanking me? Because I'm thirty minutes late?" she asked.

Joyce looked to see if she was serious, then burst out laughing. "Remember how I told you Friday that if you didn't want the guy who sent all the chocolate to the office, to send him my way?"

"Yes." Francesca even recalled telling Theo about that yesterday. That led directly to the hotter than hell kiss and confession that rocked her little world. Thankfully, after that bomb, Theo didn't say anything else about it. He made his point on how he felt for her and now she needed to decide which she wanted. The answer was still equally both. A sigh escaped her.

Joyce had dragged her by the arm to the office's front door. "Well," Joyce continued, "now you can send me either one!" Her assistant opened the door to the identical scene from Friday.

Francesca gaped and said, "I thought you took it all home with you. Flowers and chocolate."

"I did," Joyce said, happily jumping up and down. "Don't you see? They guys switched things up. This time Marcus sent you chocolate and Theo sent you flowers."

Good god. She really needed to learn to communicate better. She had told one that she didn't like chocolate and one that she was allergic to flowers, but failed to tell both, both. That just told her she needed to spend more time with each one. Which she'd gladly do.

So Monday's start wasn't as bad as it

could've been. But she needed to talk with Shane about all that happened over the weekend. There were some serious issues. She tried calling him Sunday night after she came down from the high her monster truck date provided, but he didn't answer.

For the sake of her sinuses, she had Joyce pack all the gifts and take them to her own apartment right then. Then she sent a text message to both guys thanking them. Theo she knew was sleeping, getting in from his nightshift. Marcus, she figured was nose deep in numbers by now.

Francesca was surprised Shane wasn't in the office yet. Had something happened to him that he didn't return her call last night and wasn't here this morning? Or was he avoiding her because of the events over the weekend he didn't want to talk about?

She blew a breath out and sat in her chair behind her desk. Time to think and act like a responsible adult. From the parking lot, she heard a car door close. There was no way that could've been Joyce getting back already. She lived too far away to run home and return that quickly. Then three more car doors closed and the office door opened. In walked four of her brother's friends that he hadn't socialized with much until recently.

She didn't know them very well and felt a bit uncomfortable alone with them. "Hey, guys, Shane isn't in yet."

"Yeah," one of them said, "he told us to wait here for him so we could all go together."

"Go where?" she asked. A couple of the guys scowled at the one who spoke, almost as if accusing him of something.

"To a meeting," he responded, eyeing her. "Is anyone else here?"

Not thinking much about what he asked, ready to get to work, she said no and mentioned she'd sent Joyce out on an errand. She turned to her computer monitor, putting her back to the guys. Hopefully, they'd get the idea she was busy and leave her alone.

"You know," the one who spoke earlier said, "everyone saw how you kicked Nielson 's ass Friday night at the party. It was pretty damn funny how he would let a woman beat him up. He was humiliated. About time someone put him in his place."

Half listening, Francesca nodded. She'd let slide the statement about Nielson "letting" a woman beat him. "I agree. Shane and I are going to talk about that when he gets in. There were several things that happened that shouldn't have."

"Aw now, pumpkin," the male had come to the side of her desk, "don't get mad at the

112

boys. They were just trying to have a little fun. Get some relaxation from the stressful week of work and all."

She glanced at him. "That's not what they looked like they were getting."

He chuckled and stepped closer. "Your brother is right. You are beautiful. Smart and sexy. You'd make perfect babies."

Francesca jumped up from her chair. She was more than creeped out. "Please move to the other side of my desk." He inched toward her, the grin on his face turning feral. "I won't ask again. You and your friends can wait outside for my brother." She had to back against the wall to keep out of his reach. "Don't push me, asshole." She settled into an attack stance.

His expression changed to an innocent smile. His hands came up, palms forward. "I apologize, Miss Virgata. I didn't realize I was bothering you."

She doubted that. What the hell was wrong with these people? She glanced at the other guys as they stood watching with no intent to intervene. Did they think everything was okay with this guy's actions?

"Now you know," she said. "Go outside and wait. I don't want any of you back in this office without a good reason. You've worn out your welcome."

The front door flew open and her brother barged in, headed straight for his office. Almost as a passing thought, he said, "Get away from her. She's mine." He disappeared down the hall, his office door slammed, slammed a second time, and he stomped through the office toward the front entrance. "I won't be back today, Francesca. Let's go." Then men followed, leaving the office empty and her heart racing. What the hell just happened?

SEVENTEEN

Francesca pushed the elevator button on the first floor of Marcus's apartment building. After her brother and his friends left, she didn't want to be alone in the office. The guys had really rattled her.

Their behavior was completely out of character. What had happened, or was happening, to make them so forward and...sexually aggressive? She'd locked the office and called Joyce to tell her to stay home, and away from males.

When Marcus opened his door to her knock, and she fell into his arms. She needed to feel him around her, holding and protecting her. Safe, he made her feel safe.

"Hey," he said, "what's wrong, love?" He

kissed her temple, arms tightening around her. His slight sway side to side calmed her nerves. The quiet assuredness gave her peace. Then she realized what he was wearing, or not wearing, was more like it.

She'd only seen him in coat and tie. And he looked damn hot in a suit. But now, he wore a black tank top and tight cut-off sweats. Those big broad shoulders and holy Moses, those tattoos became the focal point to stare at. Then there were his amazing legs. She'd kill for legs like his. He had a body any woman would want to climb on and ride like he was a prized bull.

"I've had a rough morning and wanted to see you," she said.

He pulled back from her, a frown on his face. "Don't tell me you don't like chocolate, either."

She burst out laughing, releasing built-up tension. She was so not expecting him to say that. "Actually, I don't. But that was the best part of my morning until now."

"What?" His confusion made her giggle more. She started to feel like herself again thanks to this man. He led her to an oversized plush recliner and settled her into his lap, laying her head on his chest. She sighed with contentment. His smell was relaxing yet intense. She was switching from one extreme to the other, both mentally and physically. All this skin and heat.

"Now," he started, "let's try this again. Tell me everything." Francesca told him about Luci's Friday night close call. Nothing about Jim the accountant. She really wanted Marcus to not kill Jim before tax season. Then she mentioned what Luci and her friends said about the strange things guys were saying. When she was finished, Marcus was not a happy camper.

"Francesca," he said, "I'm prefacing what I'm going to say with I know you're a grown woman who can take care of herself, but you're worrying me. What if your brother can't control these guys? What happens if things get worse? Are there others strong enough to round up this group if they get out of control?"

"I know what you're saying, Marcus. But nothing like this has ever happened before. Why would it now?"

"That's a good question. You need to find out what's at the bottom of this. I have some contacts that can help. They are ex-military and FBI guys—"

"Whoa, Marcus. This isn't a terrorist group. It's a bunch of Neanderthals who've gotten too big for their britches. I don't want to make a big scene and draw attention to our little community."

"I understand, love. But I'm worried about you. As I said, you can take care of yourself, but what if a group of them come at you at once?"

She thought, *like this morning at the office?* But didn't dare say it. He would blow a gasket. She did agree with him on this: she had to figure out what was causing this particular aggressiveness. She remembered the girls saying the guys talked about bringing honor to the pride. That sounded like something her brother said the other day when they had visited their father. Where had Shane gotten those ideas in his head?

He moved around in the chair, brushing his collarbone against her cheek. Mmm. She wanted to taste him. "Is this how you dress when working at home? After seeing you so formal, it's hard to see you so casual."

"I was actually working out. I don't get much exercise during the day when on a case."

"Oh," she sat up from leaning on him, "you've got a project to work on. I'm keeping you from that. I should go—"

His arms scooped her back to him. "No, you don't. You're not going anywhere."

"But you have a job—" she insisted.

"I also have this perfect woman sitting with me." He kissed the top of her head. "You're more important than anything else in my world. You come first."

Aww, her heart melted. He really liked her. And she really like him. What about Theo? Sitting in Marcus's lap was not the time to think of the "other" man. Change the subject. "So, are you close to finding the evidence for your bad guy?"

"This man, or woman, I suppose, is a piece of work. I will make sure they never get out of prison for what they've done. And the worst part is, from what I can tell, the people he's stealing from don't have a clue he's doing this. There's a ton of fake paperwork to make it all look legit. Like Bernie Madoff and his scandal."

He scooted in the big chair to look her in the eye. "Francesca, promise me one thing. If you ever get an inkling that something is off in your or the prides' bank accounts that you'll look into it. Don't let it ride, thinking someone else would never double cross you. I'm here to tell you there are not a lot of people you can trust. Only family and close friends."

He smushed her to his chest and continued. "Some people really don't care about anyone but themselves." Her stomach growled. How embarrassing. "You know," he said, "it's almost noon. How about I order pizza and we can hang out for a while? There's, uh, something I need to tell you." His look became sheepish.

She leaned away from him. "What? Is it bad? You're worrying me."

He squished her shoulders against him, tilting her head to his chest again. "No, no." He waved a hand in the air. "Just some information."

That's not what his scent told her. "May I use the restroom?" she asked.

"Uh," he looked toward the hallway, "can you hold it for a few hours?"

"What?" She swatted him. "No, I'm not holding it? What's wrong with you?"

"I'm just thinking about the immediate future. Restroom is down the hall, first door on the right." He set her on her feet, snatched up the phone, and dialed from memory. He probably did not cook much since it was just him.

Now that she was away from him, she was picking up other smells. One in particular was familiar. The closer she got to the hall, the stronger the smell got. She hurried into the bathroom for a place to think. She closed the bathroom door as quietly as she could.

There was no question. Theo was in the

apartment.

EIGHTEEN

Francesca sat on the bathtub edge in Marcus's apartment, trying to figure out why Theo was there. And hiding in a room. Did the guys think she wouldn't smell him? Wait. Was that why Marcus kept pulling her face close to his skin—to keep her from smelling Theo? What the hell? What was going on?

She narrowed her eyes then. Was this some kind of game? "Yeah, there's definitely information I need to know," she said to herself. She stomped to the end of the hall. Marcus put the phone down. At least food was coming. They could all eat after she chewed him another asshole.

"Why is Theo here?" She leaned against the sofa, arms crossed.

He sighed. "Theo," he yelled, startling her. "Theo, get your ass out here. Theo!" From a room down the hall came a crashing sound and thump on the floor. A door flew open.

"What? I'm here." Theo came running out. At least she thought it was Theo. He had his fire hat on backwards, one hand shifted into his lion's paw, and wearing only black bikini underwear with red stripes. And a massively hard cock peeking out the top. "Is the house on fire?"

He looked around dazed, like not entirely awake yet. His body was simply reacting to a stimulus. And, my god, what a body that was. Big. Buff. Strong. With enough muscles to make her whimper. There wasn't a single ounce of body fat anywhere on him. Anywhere.

Yeah, she made sure to look. She pressed her legs together, hoping to stop the wetness from seeping to her panties. Or from him knowing it was there. Her pussy tingled and lust roared in her belly. She had to suppress her tigress to keep from doing something stupid, like jumping him.

She was too shocked to react. Licking her lips was about it.

His eyes stopped on her and a big smile graced his face. "Hey, baby. What are you doing here?"

Marcus came to stand behind her and put a hand over her overly-wide eyes and closed her gaping mouth. "Theo," he said, "as you can see, I have a guest. Put some clothes on." He mumbled as he walked toward her. When he reached her, he squatted down, shoved her over his shoulder and headed back to his room.

"Hey," Marcus said, "you can't take her from me. She's my guest."

"Then get your furry ass in my room."

Francesca kicked and called out. A piggyback ride was fine, but she didn't particularly care for her ass end to be in the air. "Put you down in just a second, dear." Theo shuffled into his room and tossed her onto the bed. He then sprang into the air and spread out his arms and legs, leaping as if to squash her into the mattress. "Kamikaze!"

Francesca squealed and slapped her hands over her face. She knew he wouldn't hurt her, but it was fun to play along with him. The guy was such a goofball.

He landed stretched out beside her and they bounced. In a blink, Marcus was on her other side, same position as Theo. They both put an arm around her and snuggled their faces into each side of her neck.

For the first time since her family broke with losing her mom, she felt completely at peace, completely loved, completely turned-on.

She wasn't sure what to think. This wasn't her thing. Two guys? But then Marcus cupped her face and kissed her and she lost the mental fight with that train of thought. Before she knew it, Theo was kissing her neck, flicking his tongue back and forth.

She moaned, kissing Marcus back, sucking his tongue and matching his desire with her own. One of Theo's hands pushed at the waistband of her pants.

He slipped his hand inside and between her legs, straight to her pussy. She lifted one leg over his, giving him the space needed to play with her sex. He pressed closer to her back, his rock hard erection thrusting into the curve of her ass.

Marcus continued kissing her, his hand went under her top and up to her tits. She was a big girl and the approving grunt he gave made her that much wetter. She gripped his shoulder while pushing her ass back into Theo. This was insane. She didn't do this.

Two men at one time touching her and doing these things was not her. But it felt so right. It felt so good. So goddamned perfect.

Theo rubbed his fingers over her clit in slow circles that drove her crazy. Marcus pulled away from her lips and shoved her top up, pushing her breasts out of her bra and sucking a nipple into his mouth.

"Oh, god," she gasped.

Theo licked the curve of her neck, whispering by her ear, "I can't wait to fuck you. My cock, your lips, it's going to be fucking beautiful."

She gulped. Marcus sucked on her nipple hard at the same time Theo increased the speed of his flicking of her clit. They worked in simultaneous movements. Theo rocking his erection into her and rubbing her clit. Marcus nibbling her breasts and growling with each lick. He went back and forth between the two, making her crazy.

Tension curled at her core so fast and hard, it left her breathless. The two men working as a team to draw out her pleasure had an unexpected effect. She loved it. Her body reveled in their touch. Goose bumps broke out over her skin as she went closer to the edge. Another harsh moan struggled up her throat.

Theo grunted behind her, his erection pressing so tight at her ass she swore he was going to rip through both their clothing. Marcus sucked harder, biting and licking the valley of her breasts before moving to her other tit.

She inhaled a rough breath, digging her claws into Marcus's arm and losing her mind when Theo increased his speed on her clit. She was soaking wet and his fingers were gliding between her folds.

The two of them combined their moves again. Marcus bit down on her nipple and Theo tapped hard at her clit. The dual bits of pain sent her soaring. Fire coursed her veins and a loud scream tore from her throat.

Her pussy grasped at the fingers Theo shoved into her. The scent of both men's pheromones made her purr in contentment. She wanted more. Now. Both of them inside her. Nothing else would do.

The sound of the door bell chiming pulled her out of her sexual daze. She blinked and saw Marcus lift his head from her chest. His bright glowing eyes focused on her. He was breathing hard and having a damn hard time holding on to his human skin.

"I'll get that," he said in a deep, rough voice. She glanced down and couldn't miss the massive erection poking at his pants. Christ. What the fuck was she thinking?

Theo pulled his hand out of her pants and bit around her shoulder. The move sent shivers down her spine. That's what she wanted. More of that. But he didn't bite hard enough to mate. Just enough to make her wet all over again.

"We better go," Theo grumbled.

She pressed into him one more time before pulling away. Her tigress wasn't happy. She'd been delighted at two very strong men giving her their full attention. Making her the sole focus of their desire. Her tigress argued this was perfect. Both men should be hers because she wanted them both. But Francesca wasn't the ménage type. As it was, this was the craziest thing she'd ever done.

Damn pizza delivery.

NINETEEN

The threesome: lion, tiger, and bear, oh my! sat around the coffee table eating pizza. The two guys each had a large pizza to themselves while Francesca took a piece from each. Those two had to work just to support their food intake.

"So," Francesca said, "you two have been practically brothers since childhood."

"More than that, it seems." Theo shared a look with Marcus that she didn't understand the meaning behind. She wasn't sure she wanted to know. Not with her body still humming from both men touching her.

"So, tell us about you," Marcus said. "You're clearly looking for a mate if you went to Gerri. Are you looking to get married?

Have a bazillion babies and settle down?"

She raised her brows. Her heart slowed a little. "I would like a mate, but I don't know about marriage and kids. I have never really been around children so I'm not sure how I feel about them."

"Babe," Theo said with a grin, "You'll love kids. They're adorable and bring out the parent instinct in everyone."

Marcus snorted. "Speak for yourself."

Francesca blinked. "Don't you want kids?"

Marcus shrugged. "Yeah. I definitely do, but not a bazillion of them. I think starting with one is a good idea. Though, I know for sure two is a must." He pressed his lips into a thin line. "I wouldn't want my kid to grow up alone. That really sucks."

She nodded. "Yeah, but you'd also not want your child to have a solo crazy sibling he or she might not talk to."

Theo rubbed his jaw and picked up another slice of pizza. "This tells me she wants three kids. That's a great number."

Francesca laughed nervously. "Whoa there, Romeo. I don't know about that. I just said I don't know how I feel about kids. For all I know, I won't want any."

Both men stared at her in shock. Crap. What now?

Theo waved a hand dismissively. "Not gonna happen. I can sense your tigress is going to want a bunch of cubs herself. You just need to spend time with them." He winked. "Then you'll be all over me, begging me to give you a dozen babies."

Marcus elbowed him. "Hey! Maybe she'll be all over me asking me to make her pregnant for the next ten years."

She chewed her slice of pizza slowly. "This is a good time to ask, what happens if I don't want children?" She glanced from Marcus to Theo. "Will you not want me anymore?"

"Never!" both men said in unison.

Theo pulled his chair closer to her, as did Marcus. Both men were now squishing her from both sides.

"Listen to me, Francesca," Theo said, wiping his hand and picking up hers. "You could decide you will never want children and I will still want you. My animal and I are one hundred percent sure you're our mate." He brought her hand to his lips and kissed it, his eyes never straying from hers. "I want you. Only you. Nothing will change that."

Marcus picked up her other hand, ignoring the napkin she held and brought it to his chest. "Children would be a bonus." He met her gaze with his own unwavering one. "But they are only a small part of what we would be. You mean more to me than you will ever know. And as much as I may want children, I want you more. More than anyone. More than anything."

"And that's settled," Theo grinned and handed her another slice. "Kids are not a deal breaker for either of us."

Lord. For a second there she thought they were both trying to sell her on a relationship between the three of them. She had mental problems. That would be...so sexy. No, no, no. That would be wrong. Not what she wanted. Right? Maybe.

"Are you busy Wednesday night?" Marcus asked.

Besides her nightly TV dramas, she never had anything going on. "I could be free. Why?"

"The family gets together every Wednesday to eat and socialize for a couple hours. Would you like to go? I'd love for you to meet the family," Marcus said.

Meeting the family already. To make matters worse, it was the same family for both men. How awkward was that? Would she cause a civil war within the family, picking sides on which man she should choose? But then again, no matter which guy she picked, she'd be with the same family. Why not just get it over with?

"Sure," she said. "I'd love to meet your family."

Theo sat, chewing on pizza, not looking thrilled. "Marcus, don't you have some super important case you're working on? Shouldn't you get back to it?"

Marcus glared at him, but said nothing.

"Don't let man or my mate get in your way," Theo said. "In fact, Francesca, would you like to go to the firehouse with me and meet some of my other family?"

She nearly choked on her pizza. Her? Go to a place where the men would be freaking hotter than shit? "Sure, that'd be great. We can let Marcus get back to work then."

"Yea, great." Marcus looked to shoot daggers at his roommate.

Oh god. How was she going to get through this?

Instead of the motorcycle, Theo drove his truck to the station. After Sunday's show, she became a fan of big-ass trucks and riding motorcycles. So sitting in his decked-out Ford 350 diesel pickup truck felt almost boring. He had a lift kit high enough that her head met the door halfway.

"Is this even street legal?" she asked, being

playful.

With a seriousness she hadn't expected, he took her hand and kissed it. "Baby, I would never put you into anything I felt wouldn't be safe. Same for Marcus. His car is five-star rated crash tested. We'll keep you safe."

They pulled into the station's parking lot already filled with several big trucks. Must be a firefighter thing. Pretty kick-ass, actually.

After opening her door, Theo lifted her from the seat and slid her down his front side, his flaccid cock still a good size for her to feel. He flashed a wicked smile. Dog. Now she was all hot and bothered. He popped open the metal toolbox across the back of the truck and took out some gear, tossed if over his shoulder and grabbed her hand.

A few guys were out back of the house and whistled as they walked up. A strapping redhead wearing suspenders leaned against the brick. "Well, looky here. I'm not sure which is prettier, Surfer or his dazzling young lady friend." The man stuck out his hand. "I'm Red. Nice to meet you, young lady. A word of advice for you." He pulled her away from Theo. "I've known this kid for a long time. I suggest you run as fast and far as you can."

TWENTY

Theo huffed and dragged her back to him. "Don't listen to Red," Theo said. "He's just mad his mama got some last night and he didn't." The guys broke into laughter.

"Good one, man." Red waved him the finger. "Let me tell you what your mama did this morning." He thrust his hips out. "Me."

Theo laughed and shook his head. "Yeah, she did come home saying she met a little prick."

Red snapped off a suspender. "I'll show you little."

Francesca was jerked forward through a doorway before the big guy undressed further. Hoots of laughter followed.

"He called you Surfer. I bet his real name

isn't Red, either, right?" she said.

"Some of us have a nickname," he said, flipping his hair. "You can guess how I got mine." She smiled. She could definitely guess with his California look.

A booming voice came from around a corner. "Did I hear someone reference a female in our midst?"

"Chill, Stockholm," Theo hollered. "She's not available."

"Says who? She ain't seen me yet. Then she'll be unavailable."

Francesca laughed. She liked this unseen guy already. Then the man lumbered out. He was a freakin' giant.

"Francesca, this is Stockholm. He's a polar bear from Sweden. He's been here forever." Theo looked up at the man. "Dude, I don't even know your real name."

The bear chuckled, deep and growly. "Neither does most of the crew." He shuffled away, pulling a pack of cigarettes from his pocket. She couldn't believe it. She'd never seen a shifter smoke. With such heightened senses, she wouldn't have thought it possible for anyone to withstand.

Going through another door, they came into the main living space for the men. "Hey, Theo," one of the guys said then did a double

take. "Surfer Boy found himself a princess."
In less than a heartbeat, six other curious
faces stared at her. Being the center of
attention was not her favorite place to be.
But these were Theo's friends and she
wanted them to like her. She smiled and
waved.

Theo continued to lead her out of the large,
open room. "We'll be back in a second," he
called out. At a locker, they stopped and he
crammed his stuff inside. He took her face in
his hands and kissed her, long and deep. He
pulled back, panting. "Don't let any of the
guys rile you up. They are all great and
honorable men. We'd give our lives for each
other. That being said, if any of them touch
you when I'm not looking, haul off and kick
them in the balls." He winked.

They walked out another door to the
garage housing the big trucks. "Wow," she
said. "I didn't realize how big these things
really were." Theo opened little cubby holes
and spaces all over the truck to show here
where they kept things. She had no idea
there was so much hidden away.

On the far side of the garage, they came to
gym equipment and a few guys—sweaty,
sexy, hot, with little clothing on guys. Oh my
freakin' god. She looked away when her face
erupted into flames. At least she was in the
right place for that.

"Hey, Theo. Who you got there? Much better looking than your ugly mug." A guy spotting a bench presser hefted the bar onto the stand. He came over, wiping his hands on a towel.

"Hey, Griz. This is Francesca. She's my mate." Francesca heard that term, but didn't let it affect her in front of the guys. It kinda ticked her off that Theo assumed he knew who she'd pick. Then again, he was probably showing off for the guys. That didn't make points in her book. "Or Marcus's. She hasn't decided yet."

Griz shook her hand, his fingers completely engulfing hers. "Talk about opposite ends of the spectrum. A bean counter or adrenaline junkie? Good luck, Miss Francesca." He winked at her and smiled. "You know what, Surfer," Griz said loudly, getting the attention of others in the garage, "I think it's time for the monthly Shape Up or Ship Out."

Theo groaned. "Come on, Griz. Don't do this to me in front of my girl."

Griz pretended to whisper into Theo's ear. "I'm helping you out, man. Once she sees this, the bean counter will be adios, baby."

"Maybe, but what about the other guys here who will be almost naked in front of her?" Theo twirled her against his chest so her nose smashed into his sternum. "She's only seeing me."

Whoa, wait a minute. She jerked back and glared at him. "Are you telling me what I can and can't do?" A male snickered behind her.

Theo swallowed hard. "No, baby. Not in the slightest. If you want to look at other men, you...you..." he couldn't say it, "can."

She laughed. "No, sexy," she said, "I just want to see you in little more than those hot Speedos you had on earlier." She bit his earlobe.

His body shuddered. "You're on, Griz. Bring on all the guys."

TWENTY-ONE

Francesca stood in a circle of men gathered around the weight bench. She'd met everyone, but remembered only a few names. She couldn't believe how sexy every one of these men were. It was a female's dream. But her eyes were fixed on Theo.

She felt a bump on her hip and another woman edged her way to next to Francesca.

"Hi, I'm Kelsy. I'm an EMT with the ambulance service. It's good to see another female face around here. I get tired of looking at all these ugly males." The guys around them groaned.

"I'm Francesca. I'm here with Theo." She nodded toward him among two other Adonises, half naked. "What's this Shape Up

Ship Out thing?" she asked.

Kelsy rolled her eyes. "It's when too much testosterone builds up and needs to be released. Though I can't complain too much. It's great eye candy." She turned to the action in the circle's middle. "They battle to see who can press the most. It's a bit childish, but like I said, eye candy."

The men slapped chalk on their hands. The white powder floated in the air, giving a surreal feel with the fading sun's rays cutting through like lasers. The three guys bounced around on their toes like boxers in a ring. But all Francesca noticed was how the muscles streamlined down each of her man's legs. Cut from the hardest of stone.

Kelsy shook her head. "I must say, Red may be a bit of a country bumpkin but damn, he's got a nice ass. Curved just right for squeezing."

Francesca studied Theo. "You got it. Just right for squeezing. Both sides, actually."

"One thousand pounds," Red hollered.

"Holy shit," Francesca said. "Isn't that a lot?"

Kelsy shrugged. "Humans on 'roids have done that much before. For shifters, it's average."

Men scurried around, lifting round

weights and sliding them onto the end of a silver bar. Red lay on the bench, wrapped his hands around the bar, lifted it, pumped it twice, and set the bar back in the cradle. Cheers went up. Theo and the third man repeated the process.

Francesca blew him a kiss when he sneaked a look at her.

"Thirteen hundred," Red called. While men scattered to find the round weights to add to the ends of the bar, the three men consorted with their designated "trainer" for the competition. The crowd eased back. Chief Hinton made his away to Francesca.

"It is nice to you, Miss Virgata," he said.

"Please, call me Francesca, Chief," she responded.

"Thank you, young lady. Are you by chance related to Steve Virgata? Tiger pride, I believe."

That was surprising. "He's my uncle, brother to my mom. You know him?" she questioned?

"I do. Went to school together. Good family, the Virgatas. How's Steve doing these days?"

"He's great. After a scare with a heart attack, he took up karate to regulate his blood pressure and exercise his human form.

He teaches a couple classes a week. I call him sensei more than I do uncle."

The chief laughed. "I would've never seen that coming. But there were a lot of things none of us kids figured on growing up."

That sounded cryptic, but she also understood where he was going with that. Things had changed a lot for her since graduating and being on her own.

"Did anyone ever tell you how your uncle got that scar on his face?"

The question startled her. This man really did know her uncle, not just an acquaintance. "No. I always wondered, but never asked. You know?"

"I know firsthand. I was there."

He had her full attention. "What happened?"

The chief settled into his stance and he seemed to lose himself in memory. "Back in the summer of our senior year of high school, a group of us had gone out to Townford's lake for the day. Just being kids. Girls were on floats and the guys finding it exceptionally fun to dunk them.

"Anyways, me and Evie, that's my mate, we snuck ourselves through the cattails for a little alone time. Seemed it was more than just me and her, though. A gator had

143

wandered into the lake and decided it was hungry and wanted a piece of me." Francesca gasped. She had no experience with those animals, but they scared the shit out of her when they showed them on TV.

"The critter," the chief continued, "got a hold of my leg and dragged me from the bank into the water. Evie set to hollering, unable to do anything as I wrestled the animal best I could. Being rolled and unable to see in the muddy water, my wolf couldn't even save me.

"Long story short, if it weren't for your uncle showing up out of nowhere and gutting that monster with his claws, I wouldn't be here." He lifted a pant leg to show her the grizzly damage to his leg.

"My muscle was so badly shredded that even a shift couldn't heal it all the way," he finished.

"How did my uncle get the scar on his head?" Francesca asked.

"When he first dove in after me, he tried to free my leg from the gator's mouth. In all the thrashing and water splashing, the animal clawed him in the face with a foot. Almost took his eye and gouged out a row of flesh. But we both made it through." He stood quietly, probably recalling the terror and happiness at being alive.

He lightly slapped a hand on her shoulder.

"Yes, good family, the Virgatas." He turned toward the inside area. "Been a long time. Need to see him again. For old time's sake." The man walked away and she noticed a slight limp she hadn't before. Wow, her uncle was a hero. Why hadn't anyone ever told her that story? She'd get onto her uncle at the next practice for the oversight.

The crowd gathered for the next round of the Shape Up. The weight had been raised to thirteen hundred pounds. Red and Theo rolled through, but the last guy couldn't get the second lift the full height. Down to Red and her man. Her man? Was he?

"Fifteen hundred pounds!" was yelled from the crowd. That was half the weight of a car. Impossible! The throng chanted fifteen, fifteen, fifteen. Red looked at Theo, and he shrugged. "Why not? There's always a first." The group went wild. Men dashed away to reset the bar, others spreading the word of the record weight being attempted.

She made her way to Theo, concern surging through her. "Theo," she said, getting close to him, "don't hurt yourself. Don't do this to impress me. You don't need to. I don't want you injured because of me."

He took her face in his hands and kissed her. Whistles erupted from the onlookers. "Don't worry about me, babe. I know when to stop," he smiled, "even if I don't appear mature. This is completely a guy thing. That's why you don't get it." He kissed the top of her head.

He could say that again. She sighed and stepped back to let him and Red prepare. Kelsy somehow found her again. "You two been together long?" the woman asked.

"No, we just met about five days ago," she replied.

"Well, just so you know, you picked a good one with Theo."

"Yeah?" Francesca wondered how much this woman knew about him. Did they know each other intimately? A spark of jealousy lit her insides and she squelched it as quickly as she could. Kelsy laughed. Damn, the smell of the emotion still escaped.

"No worries from me," Kelsy said. "The guys here really love Theo, though they wouldn't put it quite that way. But each of these men would give everything for the other. Once, Smitty tried to hook Theo up with his sister. She won the local queen pageant. Drop dead gorgeous. Make you sick just looking at her, she was so pretty.

"He took her on a date so he wouldn't hurt Smitty's feelings, but he had her home before midnight with a kiss on the cheek. When I talked to her about the date, she said he was a pure gentleman, which bummed her out.

She would've loved to get her hands on him." Both ladies laughed.

"I know what she means," Francesca said.

"He's a great guy. He'll do anything for you. Even though he comes across like a total guy-idiot occasionally. But I bet once his heart is set, it will forever be."

Francesca turned to the EMT. "Thank you for telling me. That's great to hear."

"Sure." Kelsy shrugged. "Now let's see if he can kick Red's ass or not."

Suddenly, a loud alarm echoed through the garage. Groans erupted along with it. Kelsy sprinted away with the rest of the crowd. Francesca looked around, dazed by the controlled chaos. "What's happening?" Theo appeared at her side.

"That's a call, baby doll. We gotta go. Can you wait or need to go?"

"I should be getting home. I've been gone since this morning. I'll Uber it to my car. I'll talk to you tomorrow. Go." He kissed her then headed for the locker room. "Wait," she said. He stopped and looked back at her. "You would've kicked Red's butt, you know."

He smiled. "Yeah, but that's not the point, love. It's the comradery." He zipped away.

Seconds later, one of the trucks pulled out, sirens wailing. The ambulance was close behind. It was a majestic and powerful feeling watching these men and women going out to risk their lives to save others.

She saw Theo jump in the back of one of the bigger trucks. He blew her a kiss and was gone.

TWENTY-TWO

The next morning, the office doorknob rattled. Francesca looked up from her desk to see Uncle Steve peek through the window. She opened the door and gave him a hug.

"What's up with the locked door?" he asked.

"New office policy," Francesca said. She didn't explain further even though she could tell her uncle would've liked it. "What can I do for you, Sensei?" she teased.

"I came by to see if I could get a reimbursement for a personal check to pay for the lawnmower repair."

"Why didn't you use the company credit card?" she asked.

149

"I tried but it was denied," he replied. She hadn't expected that. She paid the bill in full last month. "Come in. I'll write you a check now. That's strange."

"That's what I thought. But not much I could do about it at the time." He headed for the coffeepot while she went to her brother's office for the checkbook. She tried to open the door but found it locked. Since when was he locking his door? Not a problem. A long time ago, Dad gave her a key to all the offices after she took over her mom's spot at the office. But still.

After a quick jaunt to her desk and back, she opened his office and went inside. This was the first time in a while since she'd been in there. The room was almost a disaster. Stuff was everywhere, stuff that even didn't belong in there, like Mom's fine china.

She pulled on the top drawer of his desk and took out the checkbook. Stepping around the desk, paper in the trashcan caught her eye. Final Notice was printed in red across the top of something. She snagged the crumpled sheet and stuffed it in her pocket.

Back at her desk, she wrote out the payment and tore it along the perforation. "Uncle Steve, do you know the city's fire chief?" she asked.

"Dan Peters? Sure do. Why?"

"I heard you saved his life when you guys were in school. Why hadn't Mom or you ever told us that?"

She swore he blushed. Never had Uncle Sensei Steve been embarrassed about anything. "Well, child, I did what any other person in that situation would've done. I just happened to be the one there."

"You fought an alligator, for crying out loud. That's huge, Uncle Steve." She couldn't believe he was being so modest.

He ran a finger down his scar. "I guess it kinda is. But that was a long time ago, child. Shoot, I barely remember it." He sipped his coffee and took the check from her. "Thanks for the quick reimbursement, Francesca." His eyes looked around. "No Shane yet?" He glanced at his watch. It was almost noon. "Does that boy even work?"

Francesca snorted. "Define work, Uncle. It's debatable. Seems he's always gone to meetings."

He shook his head. "I'll see you later, youngin." As their uncle pulled out in his old truck, she saw Shane in his muscle car roll in. He then stormed through the entrance.

"Shane," Francesca stood behind her desk, "we need to meet. There's a lot of things

151

we need to discuss." He walked past her without even looking at her. What the hell? She followed him. "Shane, did you hear me?"

Her brother stomped into his office, not noticing the door was unlocked. He swung the door closed, making her have to whip her arm up to keep from being hit. Now she was pissed. "What is your fucking problem, Shane?"

He spun on her. "My fucking problem?"

She would not be cowered. "Yes. Your problem. Everything is happy and smooth until you walk in and the place goes to shit."

"I have responsibilities to take care of. Stressful responsibilities. I don't just sit behind a desk and do stupid busy work. I make decisions."

Stupid busy work? Wrong thing to say. "I make this office work. Without me, you wouldn't have a company to run. I do everything here. In fact, I'd like to know what you do. What decisions do you make, dear brother? Please, enlighten me."

"I make all the financial moves. I figure out how to keep us out of bankruptcy."

Bankruptcy? They had so much money in the bank, there shouldn't even be a thought of that. Then something Marcus mentioned came to mind. "Shane, I want to take back some of the banking tasks Jim took when you hired him."

"No," he said. She waited for an explanation that she was already overloaded with stuff and didn't need the added work. But it didn't come.

"No?" she responded. "That's it? No."

"Yes." He brushed an arm through the air. "Get me some coffee and close the door behind you." He made for his desk. Boy, he was king of wrong things to say today.

She took the crumpled Final Notice paper from her pocket and smoothed it out. "What is this?" she asked as she slammed in on his desk.

His eyes narrowed. "Where did you get that?"

"Doesn't matter. Why isn't this bill paid?"

He whipped it from under her hands and stuck it in a drawer. "It's an account I decided to close."

"Account for what? Why wasn't I told about this?" she demanded.

His face bloomed red. Had she caught him doing something he shouldn't have or was it something personal he screwed up?

"Don't question me," he yelled. "I'm the prime here. You shouldn't even be working.

You should be home, taking care of children and cooking supper. Ready to spread your legs when the man who owns you gets home."

Everything in her mind stopped. He did not just say those words. Her hands balled into fists. She didn't know how to address those items that would send her into a rage without killing her brother. She'd focus on the easy points that wouldn't make her a murderer. "First off, brother, you are not the prime. Father is still in charge of the pride. Not you. Even sick, he can kick your ass out of here and send you on your own if he so decided."

She twirled around to get the hell out of there before blowing up. Prior to slamming his office door behind her, she said, "And since I'm so unimportant to this office, I'm on vacation until I decide to return. If I return."

She ran to her desk, shut and locked down everything and grabbed her purse. Relief hit her, glad Shane didn't confront her again. She would've gone bat-shit crazy karate chop on his ass. Peeling out of the parking lot, she left with nowhere in mind to go.

TWENTY-THREE

Francesca sat in her car in the parking lot of her father's medical facility. It wasn't really a nursing home or assisted living. She didn't know what to call it. But Dad could stay as long as he wanted and they would take care of any medical need he had.

She hated this place. It was the same her mother went to when she developed cancer and never came home from. She didn't want that happening with her father, too. She was too young to lose her parents. They didn't even have grandkids yet. He couldn't die until he spoiled them rotten.

The thought of having kids scared her. She didn't know how to raise them. What if they turned out bad and were mean people? What if one of her children became a serial killer, or an ax murderer? How did she handle the "terrible twos" or mouthy teens?

What happened if the baby got sick? When did she go to the doctor? She didn't want to go for every little thing and become known as one of "those" moms. But she didn't want her kids to have lasting effects from something.

Was a baby supposed to sleep on its back or front? When did you feed it? What did you feed it? When was it okay to take a baby outside or on a plane? Which stroller was the safest, which car seat? Oh god, this could go on and on. Was she really equipped to be a mom?

Her dad would know all these things. He raised her and Shane to be great people. Well, she wasn't too sure about Shane right now. He seemed deadly lately.

Their conversation played in her mind. She remembered how mad he got. Would Shane try to hurt Dad so he could have complete control over the pride? No, he'd never do that. But she'd call Uncle Steve anyway to have him come visit Dad until visitor time was over to make sure he stayed safe. She needed to be at Marcus and Theo's in a few hours for dinner at their parents' house.

Francesca pulled a chair next to the table her dad sat next to in a great room.

"Hey, Dad. You look great. Must be all the attention you're getting around here," she said.

"Well, don't know about that, but I am feeling better. Sleeping in and being pampered has its effects," he responded.

"It's probably been rough without Mom to cook full meals and clean and...other stuff, huh?" she asked.

He looked at her. She tipped her face down. Why did she ask such a stupid question?

"What's wrong, Francesca? And don't say nothing. I'm your dad. I know better."

She let out a sigh. "I don't know, Dad. I'm not sleeping well. Things aren't right. I met two great guys and have to give up one of them. Something's wrong with Shane. You're sick, and I miss you and Mom." Along with the outpour of words and emotions came the tears. She hadn't cried since Joe Reynolds broke up with her in eighth grade. God, what was wrong with her?

Dad patted her hand. "It'll be all right, Francesca. We go through things as they come, and they pass. Let's talk about the most important matter."

Francesca cringed. She wasn't ready to answer questions about what was going on in the pride—what was strange, what was wrong. Wasn't she doing her job right? Was she letting everyone down?

Dad cleared his throat, his brows drew together. "What two boys?"

Two boys? She stressed over the lives of the pride, and her dad wanted to talk about who she was dating? A huge laugh burst from her with a release of built-up emotions. She laughed with different tears falling. Some of the others in the great room looked at them. She didn't care. This is what she missed: family.

"Oh, Dad. You're too funny. You always know how to make me smile," she said.

He grinned. "That's because there is very little in this world to be sad about. Remember that." His face returned to a scowl. "Now, about the boys?"

"Dad," she rolled her eyes, "they are both great. One is an Ursave bear and the other is a Liannus lion."

"Where did you meet them?"

Oh god. Here came the third degree. "Gerri Wilder introduced them to me."

"Gerri Wilder?" He sat back in his chair. "That's fine then. You can mate whichever."

She froze. "Wait. That's it? No questions on anything?" she queried.

"If they are from Gerri, then I trust them. I trust her."

"Okay," Francesca said, "I guess you don't have a problem with women working outside the house?" Her question served a dual purpose. She kept her eyes down to not give away her deception. She'd make a horrible poker player. Staying away from Vegas was wise for her.

"Of course, I have no problem with that. Your mother worked in the office with me up till she had to stop." His head tilted. "Where did you get the thought otherwise?"

She shrugged. "Shane seems to think women should be baby makers and stay home."

"Where did he get those ideas?" Her dad looked concerned. "Your mother and I taught you kids that you could be anything you wanted. Gender has little role in this day and age. Women can do anything men can except pee their name in the snow."

Did he just say what she thought he said? Another burst of laughter erupted from her. He'd never said anything like that to her before. He was becoming less censored in his opinions as his years went by. She noticed his cheeks pink. Yeah, he hadn't meant to say that in front of her. Uncle Steve, maybe.

That reminded her, she called her uncle

earlier to come over to make sure her father was safe. Should she say anything to her Dad?

"Has your brother had any other wild hairs up his ass?" he asked.

Who was she talking to? This was not the man who just about drilled her over two guys he didn't know. It was like he was talking to a friend, not his child. Then she realized something.

He was a parent when she needed one and a friend when she didn't. Was that how it worked? He and Mom as parents taught her right and wrong through example and life lessons for her to make her own decisions as a grownup. Now when she needed advice or information, he was there as a friend to help, but not tell her what to do.

"I'm not sure about a wild hair from Shane's butt, but he's not you, Dad."

He sighed. "Just like you, darling child, we raised him to be his own person. Granted, I don't agree with the things going through his head, but there's a reason for those things. I've been here for a while now, and out of touch with what everyone is doing. With your mom gone, it's been hard.

"Being prime has kept me going. I have a responsibility to the pride to keep them safe, fed, and as happy as they can be. You and your brother pushed me to stay focused on what I had, not what I'd lost.

"Now with you two old enough to run the pride, I don't feel I'm that important—" Francesca perked up to loudly disagree with him, but he held up a finger telling her to let him finish, "so I've been pushing things onto Shane. Trying to make him ready. But maybe I've been pushing too much without being there to guide silently.

"He's trying to find himself, Francesca. You've already done that. From the start, you knew who you were. Your brother, not so much. I mentored him the best I could, but he's always worried too much about what others think.

"Give him more time. Let him figure out what he needs to be a good leader. You know all men around that age are usually jerks and idiots—so your mother told me, once or twice, when I was that age." He smiled. She could do that. As long as her dad was around, she could do anything. "Don't let your brother's ineptness worry you too much right now. He'll come around. If not, we go to Plan B."

"Plan B?" she asked, caught off guard. "What's plan B?"

Her dad looked behind her and grinned. "Well, if it ain't the worse brother in the world to finally show up and see his sick sibling-in-law."

Francesca turned in her chair to see her uncle.

"Can it, Simon. Be glad I talk to you at all with your pussy footin' around. Real tigers don't get sick." Uncle Steve winked at her. "Well, youngin, good to see you out and about. How you been?"

She got up and hugged him. "Good."

"That's good. I hope you and your dad were done talkin'. He and I got some jabbin' to do." He looked at her dad pointedly.

What did that mean? Was he going to tell her dad a bunch of bad things? She didn't want her dad to get sicker with stress.

Uncle Steve held his hug on her. He whispered, "I got this. Don't worry."

If that were only possible.

TWENTY-FOUR

On her way to the guys' house, she passed the office. There were no vehicles, which meant Shane was probably gone to some meeting for the rest of the day. She wondered what else was hidden in his office she didn't know about.

She parked in front and went in. She checked messages and went through the mail for things that couldn't wait. Then, with keys in hand, she entered his office. She hated sneaking and snooping, but like her dad and Marcus said, she needed to find out what was going on.

Lifting papers and flipping through file folders, she didn't see anything suspicious. The first two file cabinet drawers had normal stuff, but the last drawer was locked. She

163

tried every key she had and searched around for another key in his office. Nothing. Crap, how was she going to see what was in there?

A tiny pain twinkled on the end of her finger. Her cat reminded her of picking Sensei Steve's office door. But that had been more luck on her part than skill. The cat said don't be so sure. If her tigress wanted to try it again, she'd let her. A claw poked out the index finger on both her hands and the animal went to work. A minute and a few curse words later, the drawer rolled open.

She picked around the contents, looking at the weird collection of things. Bank statements, loan documents, stock certificates, lots of cash, letters from foreign banks. Receipts for expensive stuff she'd never seen like a motorcycle. What the hell was all this? Nothing looked illegal so she put everything back as it was and closed his office door behind her.

The phone rang and she hurried to her desk to answer it.

"Hello," she said.

"May I speak with Francesca Virgata, please," the voice said.

"This is she."

"Ms. Virgata, I'm Deborah from Credit Debt Agency calling to collect debt on your account with Harbor Feit."

"What? We don't owe them anything. We've always paid our bills." Outside, her brother's car rumbled up next to hers. Shit. "Deborah, can I do some research and get back with you? Our manager just pulled up and I can talk with him about it right now." She wrote down the phone number and hung up when Shane walked through the front door. His smile was feral.

"Well, that was a short vacation," he said.

"Shut your face, Shane." She pointed to the phone. "That was a collection agency calling for past due bills. I know I mark those for payment for Jim and you each month. Why aren't they paid? What the hell is going on with you and the guys all of a sudden?"

He came toward her. "There's nothing wrong with anything. That isn't being fixed anyway."

"What does that mean?" she asked.

He stepped around her desk. "That means everything that has gotten out of hand with the morals of this pride are getting back on track."

"Again," she said, "what the hell does that mean?"

"That means we're starting to take our pride more seriously. We're going to be more productive, efficient, stronger. We won't have to worry about others thinking us weak."

"We aren't weak," she replied. "Who says we are?" He moved into her personal space and she pushed him back. He grabbed her wrists and pinned them to the wall.

"We will be stronger than anyone else around. The best way to start that is to keep the pride pure bred. Men are to protect the females from others outside the pack. The women are to be willing to do their part to grow the pride."

"What is their part?" she asked.

"Whatever the men want it to be." He glared at her. She put a knee to his groin and he released his hold on her.

She bristled and stormed out the door to her car. She needed her guys, right now, more than ever before.

TWENTY-FIVE

By the time she got to Marcus and Theo's, she'd calmed down. Maybe her brother was right. Maybe she overreacted because the last person who stepped behind her desk frightened her.

The guys were downstairs waiting for her. She glanced at her watch. "Am I late?" she asked.

Both guys took one of her hands. "No, love," Marcus said. "We wanted to leave early so we could talk." He kissed her on the cheek.

"Yes, love," Theo mimicked Marcus's properness and kiss to the cheek. "We wanted to leave early so we—" Marcus slapped him on the chest.

"Shut it, moron," he said. Theo's feigned pained expression made her laugh. She hadn't been around the two together much. Last time was hot as hell though. She shuddered.

Theo leaned toward her ear. "That's what I thought about last time, too."

Francesca looked around at the expansive yard, taking in the racket of Marcus's family dinner. With food enough to feed an army, let alone a sleuth of hungry bears, the adults talked and ate, each jumping in and out of multiple conversations with ease as though second nature.

Toddlers ran wild, getting into everything they shouldn't, as their parents tried to keep them corralled, yelling for the tweeners and teens to poke their noses up from their phones and help.

"This is nothing. You should see them at the holidays," Theo joked.

Francesca laughed. "I can only imagine."

"It's great, actually. When I first met Marcus, I had no idea families actually got together like this."

She looked at him. "Aren't lion prides close?"

He shook his head. "Not like this."

She made a face. "Tigers neither. Don't get me wrong, we love each other and all, but—"

He slipped his arm around her waist and leaned in to kiss her temple. "I get it, love. No need to go there tonight."

"Go where?" Marcus asked, laughing as his nephew squirmed out from under his arm. "Stay out of the koi pond you little monster!"

Francesca watched the gorgeous toddler run off, glancing over his tiny shoulder to see if his strapping uncle followed. A soft smile tugged at her lips as she looked from the small child to Marcus. The boy had the same crooked grin and her heart squeezed thinking of what Marcus must have looked like at the same age.

"I told my mother it was a mistake to put in that pond. We can't keep him away from the fish."

Theo snorted, watching as the boy planted himself on the rock wall ready to grab at the next fish that swam past. "Look." He gave a chin pop toward the boy.

Marcus exhaled, shaking his head. "This is ridiculous. My sister would do better taking him to Alaska for the salmon run."

Francesca linked her free arm with

Marcus's elbow. "Leave him alone. He's cute." She went up on tiptoe and kissed his cheek. "Just like you."

The muscular bear growled low and lifted a hand to her cheek.

"Aren't you going to introduce me to your girl, Marcus?"

His head whipped around. "Mom...yeah...I mean, yes, ma'am. This is Francesca."

Theo cleared his throat, eyeing the big bear.

"Uhm, yeah...and you remember Theo, of course."

His mother eyed them both with their arms linked with Francesca. She inhaled, and a knowing set to her lips told them she guessed at their mutual attraction.

"I suppose roommates do tend to share everything." She smirked, chuckling at the appalled look on Marcus's face. "Don't look so surprised, son. Hilda found herself in much the same predicament and she solved the problem by opting for a ménage. It worked for her, and besides, dual-natured beings are as much their animal as they are human, with one small benefit. We are not bound exclusively by the morals of single-natured humans. We love who we want, when we want and how we want." She nodded once. "You three should think about that. You wouldn't want to end something good just because it didn't fit in a predetermined box."

She kissed her son's cheek and squeezed Francesca's hand, giving Theo a quick nod before turning to join the rest of the group.

Theo whistled low. "Your mother is one smart cookie, brother bear."

He nodded. "Yup. Sometimes too much so."

A huge splash and a loud squeal grabbed their attention, and Francesca laughed watching Marcus's sister lift her dripping son from the koi pond. The little ones were a handful, but for the first time in her life the idea of chasing around after her own left a warm fuzzy feeling in her stomach instead of a pit of panic. She glanced up at the two men flanking her and smiled to herself. Especially if her kids were as amazing as these two.

"Penny for your thoughts, love?" Marcus asked, lifting her fingers to her lips.

She smiled, opening her hand to cup his cheek. "Oh, I think they're worth more than that."

"Everything about you is worth way more than that."

"Amen, brother."

Marcus's smile was so brilliant and sexy, her heart clenched and when Theo ran his hand over her hip, her panties dampened. She was in serious danger of falling head over tail in love with both of them. Maybe Marcus's mother's idea wasn't so off the wall.

Marcus's phone buzzed and he disentangled his hand to reach for it in his back pocket. Putting a finger in his ear to hear better, he nodded. "Okay...I'll see you tomorrow then." He frowned, hitting end on the screen.

"Everything okay?" Francesca asked.

He nodded. "Yeah. I have to go to an important meeting tomorrow night. A case I've been working on for the past year is coming to a head and they need me to give my deposition." He glanced at Theo. "Sorry, dude. I guess I'm going to have to bail on the game then. She can wear my jersey."

"What game?"

"Soccer."

Before she could respond, Theo's watch beeped.

"Damn. I hate to cut this party short, but I gotta go. My shift starts in a half hour and with traffic, I don't want to be late. We've had a few fires started now that camping season is in full swing." Still with his arm around

Francesca's waist, he pulled her in for a quick kiss. "I'll call you later."

She inhaled, steadying herself against the sexual punch to her lower belly at the taste of him. Between the maternal instincts tugging on her biological clock and the feel of Theo's hard body against hers, she knew she smelled like sex on a stick to both men.

Theo growled low, his lips spreading into a smile against her lips. "Mmmmm, maybe I'll call in sick."

Francesca took a step back, swallowing the urge to drag him off to a dark corner. "You'd never forgive yourself if something happened because you stayed home to be with me."

"I got it covered," Marcus added. "Besides, you'll have her all to yourself tomorrow night."

He snorted. "True dat." Theo kissed her again and then nodded to Marcus. "I'll catch you later. Don't do anything I wouldn't."

With a chuckle, he shook his head. "That doesn't leave much, tom cat."

Grinning, he turned to leave, making his goodbyes.

Marcus slipped his arms around Francesca's waist and pulled her close, nuzzling the side of her neck. "He's right, you know."

"About what?"

"The way you smell. I may be a bear, but I know the smell of a female in heat.' He nipped the edge of her earlobe. "You're scent is making my cock is hard enough to cut diamonds."

She sucked in a breath at the low rumble of his voice in her ear. "What are we going to do about that?"

"We can go upstairs or race for the car and go home. Choice is yours. Me? I opt for upstairs because you might not make it out of the car."

She chuckled. "Haste makes waste, my sexy Ursa Major, and I don't want to waste one second with you."

Marcus's eyes shifted to a feral yellow and his nostrils flared. "Let's go."

TWENTY-SIX

The elevator doors slid open and the two walked into the empty car. Marcus pushed the button for their floor and before Francesca could utter a word, he lifted her against the mirrored wall, her maxi dress bunching around her upper thighs.

He pulled the strapless top over her breasts and buried his face in the deep cleavage, tonguing her nipples. He drew the hardening peaks deep into his mouth.

Francesca gasped, digging her fingers into his thick hair. Her legs tightened around his waist, the hard bulge from behind his zipper rough on her sensitive flesh.

The elevator pinged and he let her down from the wall, slowly. She readjusted her top

175

and stood on wobbly legs. "I think I've lost the ability to walk."

"No problem, baby." He scooped her full figure into his arms and carried her down the hall to their door.

"I can't reach the keys, love. You'll have to dig them out of my pocket," he whispered, feathering kisses against her throat.

She fumbled for the front pocket of his jeans and wiggled her fingers deep. His large, stiff cock pressed against the narrow denim and she took full advantage. Pulling the keys out slowly, she ran her thumb along the hard ridge behind the fabric, making Marcus growl. She unlocked the door and turned the handle, pushing it wide.

He stalked into the apartment, kicking the door closed before heading straight for the bedroom and depositing her on the mattress.

"Strip," he growled, licking his lips, his yellow eyes piercing through her core.

She did as she was told and wiggled the dress from her breasts to her ankles. He lifted her into his arms again and kissed her, laying her back on the pillows. His lips trailed over her mouth and throat, past her breasts to her shaved mound. On his knees, he rolled her lace panties from her hips and tossed them to the floor with her dress.

"Now you," she ordered, scrambling to her knees as well. Francesca unbuttoned his fly and slowly unzipped his zipper, reaching in to free his straining cock. She pushed his jeans past his hips and gripped his shaft, running her hand over the corded length.

Marcus sucked in a breath, and she smoothed the wet precum in her palm over his swollen head.

"You and Theo have each tasted me, now I want to taste you." She dipped her head and drew his thick member into her mouth. She moaned at the salty taste of him, letting her tongue ring the stiff ridge below his head. She took him deep, cupping his balls in her hand and massaging the tender spot between there and his ass.

Marcus dug his fingers in her long, dark hair, fisting it at the nape of her neck, urging her to take him deep, take more. She lapped and sucked, grazing her teeth over the length of him until a dangerous growl rumbled from his chest.

He pushed her back and his cock left her mouth with an audible pop. Tearing his shirt from his shoulders, he freed himself from his jeans and stood at the edge of the bed, his eyes trained on her lush curves.

"Spread yourself for me, Francesca. I want to watch you tease your slick entrance open for me."

She scooted back against the pillows and opened her knees. Her fingers slid over her belly and between her legs. She parted her slick pussy lips and ran one finger over the slippery cleft. "I don't want my fingers or yours, Marcus. I want your cock. Fill me and fuck me breathless."

He climbed between her legs and drove his member deep with a violent thrust, the force raising her ass from the bed. She cried out as his size stretched her, his ridged shaft and swollen head filling her to the edge.

Reaching down with one hand, he circled her hard nub, his hips relentless as he drove himself deeper and harder.

She cried out, her climax rolling her eyes back in her head as pleasure vibrated through her core. Shattered, she locked her legs around his waist as wave after wave crashed. The scent of her was almost too much. She was in full heat and her juice dripped down his balls. He pulled back and flipped her onto her stomach, spreading her wide from behind as he took her, letting his animal roar as he fisted her hair, riding her hard.

Francesca cried out, letting a final climax crest and explode and Marcus inhaled, his head falling back as he roared, biting back on the urge to mark her as he came, emptying his seed deep within her.

He held tight, letting every last drop pump from his body until the two collapsed forward onto the pillows. Still inside her, he cradled her close. "Was that what you expected?" he whispered.

"More," she replied, but couldn't help stiffening a bit as he nipped her shoulder from behind.

"What?" he asked, his voice confused.

"Theo. I can't help but feel like I cheated on him, though I know I didn't."

Marcus held her close, kissing the back of her neck. "He knew this was happening tonight. With the way you smelled, there was no avoiding it."

"I know, but—"

"There's nothing to second guess, love. Theo will have you all you all to himself tomorrow. It's best you have us each separately before you have to choose."

She didn't answer. Choosing was something she wasn't looking forward to and Marcus's mother's words came back, giving her pause.

"I don't want to have to choose."

He chuckled against her sweat-sheened

skin. "Then don't. Neither one of us is going anywhere and neither of us will ever force you to pick."

She rolled in his arms to face him, her eyes searching his. "You sound so sure of that."

He nodded, leaning in to kiss the tip of her nose. "That's because I am."

"Something threw me into heat tonight. It's not usual." Her eyes locked on his. "Maybe it was both of you."

He shrugged. "Maybe, but I saw the way you looked at my nephew. I think it was more. Like the two things together were a sign it was meant."

"What was meant?"

He kissed her again. "Us."

TWENTY-SEVEN

Outside the sports arena, Theo lifted Francesca from the front seat of his truck slid her down his front side, his hard-on almost instantaneous when she was nearby. She grinned up at him. "You dog," she said.

"Nah, I'm all lion for you, baby. Ready to eat you in one bite." He inhaled her delicious arousal scent. Damn, he wasn't sure he could hold on much longer without making full-fledged love to her. After sliding a black knit cap over his head and tucking his hair under it, he grabbed her hand. "Look around so you remember where we're parked." She gave him a questioning look, but didn't volunteer any answers. She'd find out soon enough.

181

People poured around them the closer to the entrance gate they got. Horns and canned blasts filled the air. Excitement electrified the crowd. Inside the stadium, the energy was palatable. Families and couples alike filled the aisles.

"I've never been to a soccer game, Theo. I don't even know the rules," she said.

"No worries, love. When a player kicks the ball into the goal I point out, you jump up and down and scream like crazy." She laughed at him. He loved this shit. Sports were his thing. After he lost his family, the only way he found to release pent up aggression was on the field. When one sports season was over in school, he moved right into the next.

They had great seats in the bottom section nearest the field. You could almost shake the players' hands. After stopping to get essentials: Cokes, popcorn, hotdogs, pizza, and grilled fajitas, they sat, ready to cheer on the team.

"Here's all you got to remember, babe," he said. "Our guys are in white, so when they control the ball, it's good." He pointed toward one end of the field. "When the ball goes into that goal, scream and shout your head off. That's it." He watched her suck a hotdog into her mouth and groaned. "Babe, you're killing me."

Francesca laughed, her mouth full of hot meat. Her eyes twinkled with life and happiness. Yes, this was the woman for him. And Marcus. Maybe. The first goal was scored and he missed it for staring at her. Eh, that was fine; some things were more important than sports. He explained the basic rules as she asked questions.

During a delay in the game when time ticked toward the end and they were up by a couple goals, he unbuttoned his pants and turned to her. "You remember where we're parked, right?" Her eyes nearly popped out when she saw him stripping.

"Theo? What are you doing?" she asked.

He scooted down in his seat. "Don't worry about me. Just head to the truck, nonchalant like." He kissed her. "Love you." Then he whipped his shirt off and leapt down the remaining stairs, jumped the railing, and ran onto the field.

He streaked across in his socks and sneakers, holding the team's pennant flag in each hand extended high in the air. The crowd went crazy. Security chased him, but those humans had no chance of catching him. He even slowed by a couple of the players and high-fived them.

Seeing this wasn't the first time he'd done this, though it had been a while back, he knew the quickest way out of the stadium and to his truck. When hitting the first row of vehicles in the parking lot, he shifted into his lion so anyone walking around wouldn't see him dashing between vehicles. Besides, if someone claimed to have seen a lion running through the parking lot, the police would throw them in jail for being on drugs.

And look at that scrumptious ass up ahead of him. Man, could he pounce on that every day and night until the day he stopped breathing. Fuck, she was hot! And she smelled delicious! As silent as a stalker, he crept up behind her, shifted, and scooped her into his arms. She squeaked as he lifted her. He kissed her hard, adrenalin and excitement racing through him.

He opened the passenger door to his crew cab and waited for her to scramble inside. The only thought in his mind was taking her somewhere and getting a taste of her. Right now. Theo slammed the door and rushed around to the driver's side, sliding into the cab.

The engine roared to life, the rumble and heavy vibration mimicking the urgency in his cock. The wheels peeled out and he turned toward a back exit, bypassing the rest of the traffic. The truck bounded over rough turf and divots behind the stadium until he pulled onto a back road. Gravel kicked up behind the wheels and the truck bed fishtailed.

"Theo! What the hell?"

He didn't answer, his fingers gripping the steering wheel tight. Just the memory of how she tasted drove his animal insane.

"Where are you going? This isn't the way home."

"Home takes too long in this traffic. I can't wait."

"Wait for what?"

He turned, feral and full of need. "To bury my cock between your pretty pink folds."

His rough voice deepened with each word. She visibly shivered and glanced down at his erection. She grinned and it was almost his undoing. He couldn't wait now.

She unclipped her seatbelt and slid across the front seat, her fingers molding to the curve of his inner thigh. He sucked in a hard breath.

"What are you doing?"

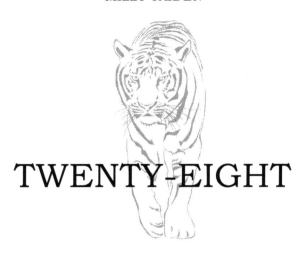

TWENTY-EIGHT

She continued as if he hadn't spoken and his mind reeled. How the fuck could he focus on driving while she touched him? Trailing her fingers over the thick shaft, she gripped him hard and ran her thumb over the head of his cock. Without a word, she dipped her mouth toward his lap and curled her tongue over the hard ridge, sucking him deep.

Theo growled, dropping a hand to the back of her head, urging her to take more. She deep-throated his full length, and he sucked in an even shakier broken breath, jerking the truck to the side of the deserted road. He shoved the gear shift into park and then reached over, pulling the lever to recline the passenger seat.

"Theo—"

She rose her head from his cock and he took that opportunity to silence her with a hungry kiss, his hands pushing her leggings from her hips along with her panties. She helped him wiggle them from her ankles. She opened her mouth to say something, but before she could utter a word, he pushed her knees apart and drove his cock deep.

A soft moan left her gorgeous swollen lips. The truck rocked with each powerful thrust and she locked her legs around his waist just to hold on. Her hips matched his drive for drive and hit for hit until the windows fogged with their ragged breath.

She raked her nails across his back and he hissed, biting down on her nipple to shove them both over the edge. She screamed his name, her body shuddering as her climax ripped through her body. His mouth watered at her wild scent and Theo threw his head back, a roar tearing from his throat as hot spurts jetted from his sex. The word MINE reverberated in his mind and his canine's lengthened, but he turned his head, forcing them to recede. Not just yet.

Entwined, the two panted in each other's arms as the urgency of their first time faded.

"Boy, you sure know how to show a girl a good time. Not even the backseat," she teased.

Theo chuckled against her throat, his voice still rough against the near miss marking. "What did you think would happen when you wrapped those luscious lips around my dick?"

"I thought you'd come in my mouth. After all, it was you who said you couldn't wait."

He groaned at the image she conjured and his cock hardened, still inside her. "Don't tempt me."

A high-pitched squeal from the console under his radio rivaled his gorgeous mate's orgasmic cries. "What the hell is that?" she asked, out of breath.

"Don't worry about it," he said. "It's a scanner that picks up calls to the fire house when an emergency comes up. I don't have to go in for a few hours. And I'm staying right here inside your hot, tight pussy until the very last second." His mouth crashed down on hers again, eager to get back to what they were doing.

He tried to ignore the voice on the scanner, but he couldn't totally block it out. His life calling was to save others, though his mate ranked above it now.

There had been a terrible wreck and vehicle pile-up on the interstate not far from them. Several engines were being called out plus a couple haz-mat teams. That probably meant a tanker truck full of gas or flammable liquid was involved.

If it exploded, a lot of lives could be lost. Like his family had been lost in the wreck and subsequent explosion that took them from him when he was a child.

"Theo," his love said, "that sounds bad. You should go to help. They need everyone they can get."

His heart burst with emotion for his mate. She understood who he was and what this job meant to him. No other woman ever got it. They only complained that he was never around at night and slept all day. This woman was perfect for them.

He kissed her and pulled out of her with a groan. "We'll pick up right here as soon as we get home. I promise." Francesca giggled and her cheeks warmed. God, she was so beautiful.

He pulled his pants on and slipped his T-shirt over his head while she continued dressing. Her worry floated on the air.

"I hope there's no one we know in the pile-up," she said. "It seems really bad."

TWENTY-NINE

At the accident site, Francesca got out of the truck as Theo pulled most of his uniform out of the toolbox in the back. There had to be a dozen cars, a semi-tractor trailer, and bus mangled in a stretch of a couple hundred feet. She'd be surprised if there were any survivors.

"Babe," he said, "please stay back where it's safe."

"You don't have to tell me twice." She had no plans on dashing into such a catastrophe. Theo ran up to one of the fire engines and pulled gear from side storage bins. First responders were spread out, pulling people through car windows and dousing flames.

The scariest situation she noted was liquid

seeping from a dent in the semi carrying a flammable substance. She could see the warning stickers and signs on the semi's carrier tank.

A flash of yellow close to the tanker caught her eye. She borrowed her cat's eyes to focus in on the long distance. Breath caught in her lungs. The color was from a bean bag, a WWF Hulk Hogan bean bag, hanging halfway out the back of a crushed Accord trunk.

Wasn't that the same bag Marcus had at the Shakespeare play they went to? How many people had a bright yellow wrestling bean in their car? It had to be him.

"Marcus!"

With little thought, she and her cat, close to the surface, sprinted past the emergency vehicles. She heard Theo call after her, but there was no stopping. No, they had a mate to save and nothing was getting in their way. Not even bossy, overprotective men.

Behind her she heard heavy thumping and clanging. No doubt, Theo was near. What she didn't know was if he would try to stop her or help her save their mate.

The Accord was tipped onto the driver's side, the roof crushed against the back wheel of the semi, another vehicle smashed against the Accord's undercarriage. It was pinned with no way to move it. Theo passed her and leapt onto the car's passenger side, which was the only access into the car. He busted the side window with his elbow and leaned in.

Francesca heard him yell Marcus's name, but didn't hear a response. *Please don't let him be dead*, she prayed. *Please*. She tried to see what Theo was doing, but had no view of the inside of the car from where she was. Then the driver of the car pushed against the underside of the Accord moved. Francesca hadn't even noticed the woman in her panic to get to Marcus.

Francesca helped the woman out of the car and to a paramedic who had reached them. Then Francesca noted that if she got to the other side, she could look in through the Accord's windshield.

In the next breath, she saw Marcus's slack face and Theo's controlled panic as he fought with the car's frame to bend the metal to be able to pull Marcus free. She also smelled gasoline.

Taking a second to analyze the situation, she saw the answer. Her eyes met Theo's. "Get out here and pick up the car. I can get him out." She then sucked in a deep breath and yelled with strength from her cat, "Red, we need you now!"

Theo stood beside where she knelt at the

side of the windshield closest to the ground. He lifted and she squirmed under the narrow opening between the semi's tire and busted driver's window. Marcus was unconscious, but his pulse was steady. Or was that her own she heard? Nope, hers was out of control. Had to be his heartbeat.

His body was at an odd angle, squished between the bent-in roof and steering wheel. She wiggled farther in, stretching up to pry him loose, but the damn seatbelt had him strapped in. Out popped a talon from her fingertip. Have claw? You can slice and dice, pick locks and slash seatbelts.

As the belt slid away, her lungs filled with gas fumes. A violent cough tore her hands from Marcus. Time was running out. Voices registered in her brain, but she kept them to the background to keep focused on her task.

Suddenly, the car lifted several inches and Marcus slid toward her. She cushioned his head from hitting the ground and grabbed him with a deadlock hold. "I got—" Toxic fuel fumes choked her again, but her fingers stayed hooked to her mate.

Hands wrapped around her ankles and dragged her from under the car. She'd have a bit of road rash on her butt, but her cat would heal that before they got back to the truck.

Next thing she knew, she was being carried. A hot flash surrounded her, then a cooler, heavy weight. She hadn't even stopped coughing yet.

The body on her raised and flipped his helmet off. Hands rushed up and down her body, and not very sexily, she might add. "Theo," another cough racked her, "I'm fine. Take care of Marcus."

He leaned down and kissed her then held her cheek to his. "Goddammit, Francesca. You scared the fucking shit out of me." He kissed her again, then pulled back to look into her eyes. She was sure she looked a mess. Her eyes watered from fumes and coughing, which meant her mascara was everywhere. Ugh, she hated that.

He picked her up and jogged toward the trucks. Men had several hoses out. One was shooting foam onto a mangled mass of black, burnt metal. Her heart skipped. If Marcus had been in the car when the explosion went off, there would've been nothing left of him.

The implications of what she saw hit her. Her body began to shake uncontrollably. Theo held her tighter. "You got him out, baby. You saved him. You're safe with me. We're all safe." He kissed her forehead.

The next hour her brain didn't register from going into shock. She knew she was in the ambulance with Marcus on the way to the hospital. Kelsy talked soothingly to her and cleaned her up, promising that Marcus would be okay. She did good.

THIRTY

Marcus felt a warm hand in his. Beeping sounds around him were irritating until he realized the sound matched the beat of his pulse. His eyes opened. He was in a hospital room. His bear replayed all that happened. If they had a place to shift then it could finish healing Marcus's human form. But he wasn't too bad right now, if not.

The warmth in his hand was from the woman he loved. She sat in a chair next to his hospital bed, asleep. Besides a few smudges on her face, she looked fine. Her eyes popped open, meeting his. She hopped to her feet.

"How are you feeling?" she asked. "You scared the crap out of me and Theo."

He ran a hand through his hair. "I scared myself, too."

"Did you see what happened? Did someone wreck in front of you?"

He replayed the event in his head. "Yes, but I swear, it was intentional."

"What do you mean? Someone caused the accident on purpose?" The worry in her eyes told him she really cared. He loved this woman. Was it too soon to say it? The door to the room opened and Theo walked in. He'd showered and was in the clothes they went to the game in.

"Hey, bro. Good to see you around. You feeling all right?" Theo asked.

"As good as can be expected. I need to shift to get rid of the lingering aches, but other than that, I'm fine," he replied. "Police have much to say about the scene?"

"Not a lot by the time I left. They just started to interview people," Theo said. "What do you recall?"

"I was getting ready to tell Francesca. I'm driving sixty-five in the four lanes of interstate traffic heading back into town, minding my own business, and a guy pulled up in the lane beside me. He looked at me and smiled. I didn't pay much attention to him, not wanting to get into a road rage incident with a hothead.

"He speeds ahead and when he passed a car in front of a bus, he slammed on his breaks, turning almost sideways in the road. The car and bus swerved, but the semi behind them couldn't do much.

"Before I joined the pile up, I saw the guy speed away. Not stopping to even lend a hand."

When he finished, neither Theo nor Francesca said anything. Both were as speechless as he was.

"You need to give the police a description of this guy. He sounds too dangerous."

The door opened again, and a nurse walked in. She smiled when seeing Marcus awake. "Ah, good. I'll tell the doc you're awake." She took his vitals and wrote on the clipboard. "Everything seems normal. You can probably go home tonight if you want."

Marcus nodded. "I want."

"I'm off the rest of the night to take you home and make sure everything is okay," Theo said. The nurse left the room. Theo looked at an exhausted Francesca. "You're staying with us. After what you did tonight, we're not ever letting you out of our sight again."

Marcus frowned at her. "What did you do?

Wait, you didn't streak across the soccer field with numb nuts, here, did you?"

Theo busted out a laugh. Francesca was surprised. "How did you know he did that?" she asked.

Marcus rolled his eyes. "I heard it on the radio on my way home."

Marcus walked into the living room, yawning. He stretched, wincing.

"You okay?" Theo asked, putting the top on the blender at the adjacent kitchen counter.

"Yeah. I'm still a little sore from the accident, but it's nothing to worry about. Like second day soreness after skipping the gym."

TV remote in hand, Francesca glanced at him from her place on the couch. "Shifters don't get second day soreness, Marcus. We speed heal. It's why you and I are here instead of on side-by-side slabs in the county morgue."

"Jesus, Francesca..."

She shrugged. "Just saying. We're luckier than most."

Theo winked at her, sparing a glance for

Marcus. "That we are."

"What are you watching?" Marcus plopped down on the couch, grabbing the remote from her hand.

"TV Land Classics. Three's Company."

"Hey now! That's a thought." Theo winked, handing each of them a fresh smoothie the color of grass. "Bottoms up. It's what I drink after a hard night at the firehouse."

Marcus wrinkled his nose. "What is this?"

"What do you think, Boo Boo? Veggies and herbs. It'll help heal whatever your quick shifts missed after the accident."

"Smells like catnip and bears don't do cat crack." Marcus put his glass on the coffee table. He glanced at the television and shook his head. "Why are we watching this?"

Francesca sipped her smoothie. "There's nothing else on. What? Not in the mood for classic sitcom TV, Marcus?"

He laughed. "Classic sitcoms sure, but this one's got it all wrong. First off, they've got two girls and one guy. Statistically that never works. Trust me, I'm an accountant and I know statistics."

"So what would work, then? Statistically, I mean." She knew full well where the clever bear was steering the conversation.

It was only a matter of time before the two hunky shifters asked her to make a choice. Problem was she was equally and as deeply in love with both men.

"I think you know the answer to that, Francesca." Marcus took her free hand and lifted her fingers to his lips.

Theo nodded, slipping onto the sofa as well. "One word. A simple yes is all it will take to get us off this merry-go-round." He took the glass from her hand and put it on the table before lifting her wrist to kiss the tender underflesh.

The feel of their lips sent heat skittering across her skin and she closed her eyes. This was crazy.

Yeah, crazy delicious.

The chorus to "Torn between Two Lovers" played in the back of her head and she sighed. Feeling like a fool... yup, the lyrics to the old seventies classic couldn't be more right. Loving both men was breaking all the rules. Except rules were the last things on her mind right now. Not with both men and their amazing bodies close enough to taste.

Theo and Marcus were everything to her, and she to them. She knew what they wanted. Both had made it clear they wanted her for their mate. Theirs. As in share and share alike.

Somehow the two men had come to terms with the possessive nature inherent in all male shifters and were willing to play outside shifter custom, each forsaking individual claim.

She was dual-natured as well, so she knew the kind of sacrifice this meant, and the strength of their conviction and love boggled her mind.

Now the choice was up to her.

The enormity of the decision hit her square in the chest and she pulled her hands free of theirs and pushed herself from the couch.

"I need a moment."

THIRTY-ONE

"Francesca—" Marcus called after her, but the bathroom door shut without a response.

Theo got up and stalked to the closed door. "Francesca! Open the door, baby."

Marcus flanked his side and knocked as well. "Yeah, open up, love. Whatever hot head said or did, he didn't mean it."

"Hot head? I'm a fireman, pencil boy. The only fires I start are between Francesca's legs. Maybe she didn't like the spit bath you were trying to give her. Maybe you should leave the tongue action to the big cats, brother bear."

"Spit bath! At least I don't need my fingers to count, you feline Neanderthal! Having a long fire hose does not a good mate make."

"What the hell does that mean? I got news for you, Yogi. You're not smarter than the average bear, so shut up if you have nothing of value to say. Francesca is stressed enough."

She leaned on the granite counter and bit the inside of her cheek at the big lugs and their bickering. They were like the male equivalent of sister wives. Leave it to shifter men to get in each other's faces instead of asking what was wrong. Neither had a clue she was willing to give this threesome a chance.

The last twenty-four hours proved not only how much they cared about her, but each other as well. How well they worked together as a loving unit. She needed a moment, not because she was unsure, but because she didn't know how to tell them.

Francesca exhaled a quick breath. Theo was right about one thing. Not telling them was stressing her out, so she walked across the expansive bathroom and stepped down into the sunken shower and turned on the spray.

A hot soak and warm jets were just the ticket. She looked at the long bench that followed the sides and back wall of the large tiled shower. Her sex throbbed thinking about the guys and what they would look like straddling her there. She smiled to herself.

It was time.

"Francesca, please! The last thing we want is for you to feel pushed."

With a smirk on her face she stripped, kicking her clothes behind the door. She flipped the latch and the bathroom door snicked open, and she waited for their mutually stunned expressions as the door creaked wide.

"Francesca, we—" Theo began, but his words fell to a dead stop.

Marcus stood silent, licking his lips.

Moving one hand to the back of her neck, she rolled her head. "I thought a hot shower would help loosen these knots in my shoulders, but now I think a massage while in the hot spray would be a better idea. What do you think?"

The two guys exchanged glances. "Who did you mean?"

She slid her hand down from her neck and over her breast. "Both. I choose both of you."

"Are you saying what I think you're saying?" Marcus asked.

She nodded with a grin. "Yes. Three is for me."

In seconds, Theo scooped her up in a fireman carry and stepped down into the shower, clothes and all. Marcus stripped, leaving a trail of clothes as he followed on their heels.

Theo's mouth took hers, letting her down in the warm jets as he tore his shirt from his shoulders. Naked, Marcus circled behind, slipping one arm around her waist as he kissed the back of her neck, his free hand roaming the full curve of her ass and between her legs.

She moaned, breaking her kiss with Theo to watch him strip from his jeans. His long corded cock jerked free as he pushed the wet denim to the shower floor, kicking the sopping pants to the corner.

He took her mouth again, his fingers working her breasts, kneading the fleshy mounds, his thumbs grazing her nipples until they crested hard and stiff.

Francesca reached around and wrapped her hand around Marcus's thick shaft and he sucked in a breath as she slid her long fingers over the corded mass. She worked Marcus as Theo sunk to his knees, pushing her legs wide. He buried his face in the soft wet down, spreading her pretty pink pussy lips apart to tongue her clit.

Theo slipped three fingers deep, curling

them to work her spot as he sucked her hard nub. Quick and delicious, her inner walls spasmed as she came, the flood unexpected, making her head drop back between her shoulders.

Marcus claimed her mouth, his soapy fingers circling her tight hole while his other hand stroked her breasts as her climax crashed. He rode the wave, buttering her ass, circling her rim before sliding his fingers slowly inside. She groaned, but then tensed at the feel of Marcus's bulging head replacing his fingers against her snug entrance.

"Relax, love. Close your eyes and come with us," Marcus whispered as he walked her backwards toward the bench.

"...and come you will. Again and again," Theo added, kissing her as he helped guide her steps.

"Do you trust us?" Theo asked.

She nodded with a sigh.

"Good, then let us lead you where you've never gone before."

The fear of the unknown sent adrenaline coursing through her blood and Theo inhaled, cupping her pussy. "Welcome to the border of pleasure and pain. The place where we serve you...only you."

Marcus sat on the bench, and Theo spun

Francesca around to straddle him. "Ride'em, cowgirl," he said, slapping her ass.

She hissed at the sting against her wet skin, but lowered her slick sex onto his full, jutting cock. He filled her, stretching her wide as she took him deep.

"Milk him, honey. Let me see you ride him, grind him. Let Marcus make you come so you're ready for me." Theo stood at her back, his thick member pressed into her spine as he whispered into her wet hair.

Marcus sucked her tits, laving and nipping the stiff peaks as she rolled her hips, drawing him in and out. A feral growl formed in her throat and she threw her head back in a tiger's cry, her body rigid as she came hard.

Holding her waist with one hand, Theo jerked his cock until the moment was right. Marcus pulled Francesca forward, the motion lifting her ass prone and Theo spread her cheeks, double stuffing her from behind.

The sensation of both men riding her stole her breath and Francesca squeaked, her body stretched and vibrating with pleasure, her legs boneless as Theo and Marcus filled her.

She cried out, her final orgasm ripping through her, robbing her of coherent thought.

"You're ours, Francesca. You belong to us and we belong to you," both men growled, their voices rough and gravely as they jockeyed the line between feral and human. In that moment, pain scored her flesh, the sharp sting of claws and fangs digging into her shoulder and the back of her neck as both emptied themselves deep within her.

She slumped forward, too weak and too happy to move, and they cradled her body, holding her as though they would never let her go.

"Forever, love," Marcus whispered and Theo nipped her earlobe in agreement. "With us, three will never be a crowd."

THIRTY-TWO

Francesca and Theo sat at the kitchen table in the apartment while Marcus made pancakes for breakfast. He said they were his specialty. She'd see. If these guys could cook, she'd keep them both. Who was she kidding? She was keeping them anyway.

"So, Marcus," she asked, "what was so important at your meeting yesterday that they made you miss the game?"

"The current case I've been telling you about, they had news. One thing was it turns out it's a female who's been doing all the stealing and fraud. First case for me with that. It's usually a guy."

Francesca sighed. "Unfortunately, women can do just as bad as men."

"Women can be downright vicious," Theo said. "I do my best never to cross one of you." He smiled at her. "Of course, I'll cross you, preacher-style you, doggy you—"

"Jesus, Theo," Marcus complained, "can you be any more lewd?"

Theo's smile widened. "Sure, I can—"

"Here." Marcus flung a pancake at him. "Fill your pie hole with this." And Theo leaned to the side and caught it in his mouth. Coffee almost went out her nose, she laughed so hard. "As I was saying, there was a large withdraw from the company's bank account the other day and the IRS was planning yesterday to move in today and take her down."

"Damn, that sounds serious," she said.

"Big time. They'll spend the day tracking her by her phone in case she meets someone to exchange something with the money or whatever. Then they'll do their thing."

"Are you ever involved in that part?" she asked.

"Nah, too much excitement for me," Marcus replied. "I stick with the numbers."

Theo finished up the dry pancake and asked, "Do you know who the woman or the company is? Are they local?"

"No, and I don't ask either. I only know the

code name for each project. This one is called the Virgin Case."

Theo snorted and pulled butter and syrup from the fridge. "Nice name. I'm guessing it's not the dude who owns the record company or the airline."

"That would be a little obvious, Theo," Francesca mentioned as she got up to set the table. Theo's phone rang and he pulled it from his back pocket.

"Hey, Chief," he said, then paused. "Yeah, we'll stop by the police department this morning...he's as good as you can expect from a bean counting bear." He laughed. "See you tonight." Theo set his phone next to his plate. "Cops want your statement of what you saw happen. They have some photos for you to look at while we're down there."

"You guys can do that while I go home," Francesca said.

"I don't think so," both guys said at the same time.

"What? I don't need to go with you. I don't have anything to add. Besides, I need to talk with my dad." The things Shane said to her the other day bothered her a lot. The females of the pride were not going to do what the men told them to when it came to sex, mating, or anything. Something needed to be done.

After several minutes of arguing who was going where and when, Francesca was on her way home to pack clothes to stay several nights with the guys. Though nothing official had been arranged, plans for their future together had begun. She'd never been so happy in her life. Who would've thought she'd find two men who loved her with their entire heart and soul.

She pulled into the drive to her cottage home and got out to get the mail. Pulling her phone from her back pocket, she texted the guys that she made it home fine and not to worry about her. She'd see them in a few hours. She slid the phone back into her pocket and fished out a couple days of junk mail from her box.

After getting inside and locking the door behind her, she tossed the mail and bills on the table and headed for her room. She'd have to sell this place, but that was fine. There was no emotional attachment.

A scent that shouldn't have been in her house stopped her. Nielson. She turned in the hall to see him come out of her guest room, leveling a punch to her face. Her cat fought to keep her conscious and aware of her surroundings. She couldn't escape if she didn't know where she was.

"Joke's finally on you, bitch. No woman shows me up and tells me what I can do."

Her vision swirled, but her hearing was solid. Nielson was not happy; in fact, he sounded a bit psychotic. "Fuck little Luci. I got the alpha bitch, and you, bitch," a sharp pain ripped through her ribs as his boot smashed into her, "are never going to shut your legs.

"When I'm done with you, everyone else can have their turn. You'll breed the next generation of pussy power for your brother and he'll be so damn happy the pride is growing that he won't give a shit that you're locked in the alpha house instead of prison." He lifted her over his shoulder, furthering her painful breathing.

"Your brother is so pathetic. Too worried about what others think of him. He's a follower, which is fine to me. I will lead this pack as soon as the old man dies."

Even if her brother was a pansy, no one messed with her family. Yet dizzy from the hit, she fisted her hand and kidney punched his back, sending them both to the floor. He rolled onto his side, writhing in pain; Francesca dragged herself toward the door. If she could get away—a sharp pain cracked her skull and darkness took over.

THIRTY-THREE

Francesca jarred awake. She was in a vehicle by the sound of it. Her cat helped her remember what happened. Nielson had abducted her. And the man was bat-shit crazy. Who the hell did he think he was?

Coming into their pride and thinking he could push her brother around and take over. But with her father sick, she understood how the deranged asshole thought this place was ripe for the picking.

He said the same thing that Shane did about power and prestige. Had Nielson fed her brother and her brother's friends all that crap? Turning her trusting sibling into a paranoid bootlicker with minions to do as he told them?

But what did the bastard mean about her being locked in the alpha house instead of going to prison? Her to prison? Why, for what?

Pain shot through her head. She had to focus to get out of here. She could shift and try to pry through the metal. She'd have to pound her way out, and he'd hear that from the front of the car. A vibration buzzed her butt cheek. Her phone! The fucking idiot locked her in his trunk with her phone in her pocket.

She pulled it out. There was barely any light for her cat to see by, but it was enough. Theo had texted her about something. She'd worry about it later. She texted back. If she called, Nielson would surely hear with his shifter's help.

She sent a message for help, but had no idea where Nielson was taking her. He mentioned locking her in the house with Shane. That was as good a place as any. The car stopped. Shit. Time was up. She typed prime house and tapped Send to Theo. Hopefully, he understood what she meant. She dialed 9-1-1 and slid the phone back in her pocket. The trunk lifted and she closed her eyes.

Light hit her face and she tried not to flinch to give herself away.

"Good, the bitch is still out." That was one of the guys with Nielson in the clearing with Luci at the party. How many more had Nielson talked into going with his plan? What did he promise them? Sex, money, power? What else?

"Bring her inside," Nielson ordered. She was picked up and carried roughly. Now would be her chance to get away, if she could pull herself together enough to shift. But both guys would have her confined before she busted out a whisker. If she yelled for help, the 911 operator should hear her.

Sucking in a quick breath, she screamed, "Help! I'm kidnapped. Tiger house—" Another pain pierced her cheek and her head snapped to the side.

"Shut up, bitch. Who you yelling to? The trees?" Nielson slapped her again and the guy carrying her almost dropped her. "Put her on her feet."

The guy obeyed but her knees gave. Nielson wrapped his hand in her hair and dragged her along the gravel driveway toward the house. She tried to defend herself, but he was wise to her fighting abilities and was ready.

He sent a swift kick of his boot to her stomach. "Settle down, bitch. This will be over shortly and you'll spend a long time recuperating on your back on a bed." He laughed.

When taken inside, she immediately smelled the familiar smells of the house she grew up in. She was home, but not safe.

His hand still wrapped in her hair, he launched her forward into the living room. "Chain her up on the floor here. I want to keep an eye on her. Make sure if she tries to shift that all her legs pop out of joint." She rolled to a stop against a wall and hands grabbed her.

She heard several female gasps. As she fought the men binding her, she saw several other pride females, including Joyce, Luci, and her friends restrained and sitting along the wall next to her.

"What the fuck is going on?" Shane came into the room. "You bastard," he yelled at Nielson. "You said she would go to jail and not be part of this. Her being here is not the plan."

Plan? Her brother was in on a plan with this cocksucker? And there was that word "jail" again.

Nielson crossed the room and slapped Shane across the face. Her brother cowered. "I say how this game is played and the rules have changed. If she would've gone quietly like you said she would, then things would be the same. But NO ONE embarrasses me like she did. She will pay for that. And so will you if you don't play along."

Her brother backed toward the patio doors. "I've had enough of you. You've told nothing but lies from the beginning. You said you could make the pride the most powerful in the country. That others would bow down to us, no longer bully us. But that's all you've done, been a tyrant. Spent our money, raped our women—"

"And what are you gonna do about it, pussy boy?" Nielson stalked toward Shane. "Shift and fight me?"

"Yes, I will, you son of a bitch," Francesca shouted. She could fight. "Let me loose and they'll see you lose to a woman again, you fucking wimp." Oh, that pissed him off. He stomped toward her. She tried to sit up, but with her arms and legs cattle-tied behind her, she had no chance.

She watched as Shane leapt at Nielson's back, claws forming midair. Then she watched in horror as Nielson swung around, his arm extended with a gun in hand. A gun? What kind of shifter used a weapon like that?

It did the trick, though. The first bullet hit her brother fully in the chest. His momentum carried him forward into Nielson. The second shot went wild and smacked into the fireplace, cracking the gas logs. The far side of the house exploded into a plume of flame.

THIRTY-FOUR

Marcus yelled into his phone and Theo drove like a bat outta hell toward the tiger pride's prime house. They hadn't been there before, but GPS in the truck would get them there.

"I don't know what kind of help is needed," Marcus yelled. "Get everything out there now!"

Theo hung up from talking to the chief several minutes ago. Fortunately, the firehouse wasn't waiting around for confirmation of necessity. They were on their way with full artillery, threat of fire or just needed shifter-manpower.

Overhead, several helicopters buzzed by.

"Choppers?" Theo questioned. "Who has

black helicopters?"

Marcus snorted. "The only ones I know who have those are the government." They watched as the whirly birds headed around the side of the mountain, the same direction they headed. There was only one community out here that had people.

"Marcus," Theo started, "call your boss and ask him for the name of the woman in the Virgin Case. Now that I think about it, virgin and Virgata are really fucking similar."

Normally, Marcus would've laughed at that thought from his roomie. But not this time. He raised his phone and saw there were no bars for reception. "Fuck. No signal here. We have to get closer to the town."

Coming around a curve, Marcus noted a shadow of smoke in the air. They must be getting close if they were seeing chimney smoke. After another curve, there was more gray floating up. He got a really bad feeling in his stomach.

"Theo, what do you make of that dark haze? Huge ass campfire, by chance?" he asked.

Theo squinted and stepped on the gas. "Too small for wildfire, too big for bonfire. We have a contained house fire. And huge-ass would fit."

Crossing town limits, they didn't need the GPS to lead them on, they followed the smoke coming through the trees. A couple more turns took them into the forest and to the fire's source. Big red engines and water trucks blocked the front of the house engulfed in flames. Both guys jumped out and headed toward the scene.

Seemed others in the community had arrived and were helping with those coming from the house. There were several men, but most were females. Marcus stopped one the girls.

"Was Francesca inside? Where is Francesca?" The girl's face was smeared with soot and tears.

"She was there, but I don't know where she is. He had her chained up." He wanted to ask who, but that wasn't important at the moment. Overhead, the chopper floated, hanging back from the smoke. Marcus read the big yellow FBI letters on a jacket.

"No, this can't be happening. This can't be right," Marcus mumbled.

Theo looked up at the helicopters. "What?"

"We have to find Francesca now. They are going to arrest her. Or shoot if she resists."

"What?" Theo shouted.

"I'll explain later." Marcus took off.

"Francesca!" They searched through the chaotic mess of first responders and smoke. "Francesca!" Theo stopped men and asked if they'd seen her. No one had. That meant she had to be in the house.

"Let go of me, prick," Francesca shouted as Nielson carried her through the woods.

"Not on your life, bitch. You're my ticket out of here if things get any worse," he huffed and slid down a slope. "I should just fucking gut you for how you've fucked this up. Never has anyone caused me so many fucking problems. And this place was gold."

"You are an idiot if you think you could've taken over this pride. My people would've figured out your plan and shaved off your balls with a dull knife."

"Shut up!" he yelled and pitched her off his shoulder. She landed with a teeth-jarring thud. A helicopter whooshed by overhead. Nielson looked up through the trees tops. "Fuck!" He dragged her off the ground and continued down the hill toward the road.

"You know they're going to get you, right?" Francesca intended to dig whatever jab she could into him to slow him down. Whoever was in the helicopter, he obviously didn't like.

"Shut up!" He threw her again and she slid through the trees and into a ditch alongside the road. They were in the open. Hopefully, someone would drive by, see them, and call 9-1-1.

She waited for him to pick her up again, but instead, she heard a bellow and saw a giant bear swiping at the bastard. She'd never seen a bear that big before in nature. Then it dawned on her? "Marcus!" The bear turned toward her. Nielson pulled his gun. Not again, please, not another death of a loved one.

Before the gun fired, a flash of gold slammed into Nielson, sending him sprawling onto to the asphalt. A beautiful lion crouched next to a tree, its tail whipping side to side. Thank god, Theo.

Nielson got to his feet, gun aimed at her. "Either of you make one move and I'll put a bullet in her head where her pussy can't do a damn thing to save her." The guys held their ground. He lifted her from the ditch by her arm and positioned her in front of him. "Now, she and I are continuing on and you both are going to sit right there if you want to see her alive."

The bear shifted into her gorgeous Marcus. "You're the prick who caused the accident that almost killed me."

Nielson brightened. "Ah, so you're the one who's been following me for years with the FBI. Nice to meet you, Agent Dumb Fuck. We finally meet."

"Hollowman?" Marcus said. "Since when did you cut your hair? When you discovered you were almost done suckering the old and defenseless out of their money? All the millions you stole, yet here you are broke and limp dicked." Marcus shook his head. "So sad. You're a failure, after all."

Hollowman smiled. "I'm the one with the gun pointed at your mate's head. Who's a failure now?" Marcus's eyes settled over Hollowman's and her shoulders.

"Um, I'd still say you are."

The chopper peeked from around the mountain's side, with a sniper setup through the open door. Theo sprang from his crouch toward her and Francesca ducked her head as a shot sounded from the helicopter. Hollowman's head snapped to the side and he fell toward the cliff side of the road. He still had a grip on Francesca.

She tried to twist away before he rolled over the side of the cliff, but he held on even in death. She squeezed her eyes closed, not ready for whatever happened next. And she wasn't ready, for she found herself in the tight grasps of two gorgeously, naked men holding her between them. Where she was always meant to be.

EPILOGUE

Francesca, Marcus, and Theo sat at a picnic table in the tiger community's park. Marcus's family gathered around the grill as usual while the kids played on the playground equipment. Theo's firehouse crew played cornhole and horseshoes, and the tiger pride mingled throughout, meeting their new prima's family and friends.

"So," Gerri said, "this Nielson guy was actually Hollowman that Marcus and the FBI had been looking for."

"Yes," Francesca said. "All the evidence of what he was planning to set me up to take the fall was in Shane's office."

Marcus added, "It was Hollowman's MO all the way. He'd setup others to take the fall for the money he stole."

"Did he really try to set up a breeding scheme in the pride?" Gerri whispered.

"That was his twisted, sadistic plan he fooled my brother into believing," Francesca replied. "Every chance they had, Hollowman and his minions would target a girl, try to get her drunk or drug her long enough for him to get his rocks off. His excuse was he was making the pride stronger by increasing its population tenfold. Disgusting that my brother paid him for this strategy.

"What my dad and I never knew was that Shane was bullied badly in school when he was younger. That made him the person he is. I think in the end, Shane really did want to protect the pride, but this bastard got my brother in his grasp and used the opportunity." Francesca sighed. "When Shane and Jim get out of prison, I'm sure they'll be welcomed back with open arms. I will welcome them, anyway."

"Did Hollowman get that young lady pregnant in your pride?" Gerri asked. "Is there any way I can help her?"

"I'll let Juliette know." Francesca took Gerri's hand. "You truly are an amazing person, Gerri."

The blushing lady waved away the compliment. "Hush, child. It's just what I do."

"Yeah, but Gerri," Francesca said, "when will it be time for you to get a mate?"

"Don't worry about me," Gerri grinned. "If I'm up to it, one of these days. As for you..." Gerri's brows rose and she winked.

She leaned in to Gerri's side while the men were busy talking. "Thank you for setting us up." She cleared her throat and stared at Gerri's eyes. "Did you know we'd end up together?"

Gerri gave a wide grin. "Oh, yes. You three are not the conventional triad, but you are a triad nonetheless. A perfect one. And those children are going to love having two daddies."

The men's heads jerked to them, both smiling from ear to ear. "This time around, the baby scents like both of us," Marcus said.

"So we aren't really sure which one of us helped father her."

Gerri gave a loud chuckle. "Even better. She will teach you both that you're her daddies and who fathered her doesn't matter. Does it?"

"No," they said at once. "We're a team. Always have been. Always will be."

Gerri nodded. "Good. Besides, that girl scents like both of you so I can't tell either who fathered her. It's more important that you both love her like your child because for all you know, you both did it."

Francesca knew deep in her heart that the reason her baby scented like both men was because she'd be both their little girl. Eventually, they'd both father her kids, but right now they needed to be a father team. And her baby would teach them that.

"We both love her already," Marcus said.

"She's our baby. All our children will be," Theo added.

Francesca smiled at her men. "I love you."

Marcus picked up her hand and lifted it to his lips. "I love you, too."

Theo came around and planted a kiss on her lips. "I love you, sweetheart."

"Looks like my work here is done," Gerri said.

Francesca turned to Gerri again. "Wait. So about finding you a mate..."

THE END

ABOUT THE AUTHOR

New York Times and USA Today Bestselling Author

Hi! I'm Milly Taiden. I love to write sexy stories featuring fun, sassy heroines with curves and growly alpha males with fur. My books are a great way to satisfy your craving for paranormal romance with action, humor, suspense and happily ever afters.

I live in Florida with my hubby, our boys, and our fur children "Needy Speedy" and "Stormy." Yes, I am aware I'm bossy, and I am seriously addicted to iced caramel lattes.

I love to meet new readers, so come sign up for my newsletter and check out my Facebook page. We always have lots of fun stuff going on there.

SIGN UP FOR MILLY'S NEWSLETTER FOR LATEST NEWS!

http://eepurl.com/pt9q1

Find out more about Milly Taiden here:

Email: millytaiden@gmail.com

Website: http://www.millytaiden.com

Facebook:
http://www.facebook.com/millytaidenpage

Twitter:
https://www.twitter.com/millytaiden

If you liked this story, you might also enjoy the following by Milly Taiden:

Sassy Mates / Sassy Ever After Series

Scent of a Mate *Book One*

A Mate's Bite *Book Two*

Unexpectedly Mated *Book Three*

A Sassy Wedding *Short 3.7*

The Mate Challenge *Book Four*

Sassy in Diapers *Short 4.3*

Fighting for Her Mate *Book Five*

A Fang in the Sass *Book 6*

Also, check out the Sassy Ever After Kindle World on Amazon

Shifters Undercover

Bearly in Control *Book One*

Fur Fox's Sake *Book Two (Coming Soon)*

Drachen Mates

Bound in Flames *Book One*

Bound in Darkness *Book Two*

Federal Paranormal Unit

Wolf Protector *Federal Paranormal Unit Book One*

Dangerous Protector *Federal Paranormal Unit Book Two*

Unwanted Protector *Federal Paranormal Unit Book Three*

Black Meadow Pack

Sharp Change *Black Meadows Pack Book One*

Caged Heat *Black Meadows Pack Book Two*

Paranormal Dating Agency

Twice the Growl *Book One*

Geek Bearing Gifts *Book Two*

The Purrfect Match *Book Three*

Curves 'Em Right *Book Four*

Tall, Dark and Panther *Book Five*

The Alion King *Book Six*

There's Snow Escape *Book Seven*

Scaling Her Dragon *Book Eight*

In the Roar *Book Nine*

Scrooge Me Hard *Short One*

Bearfoot and Pregnant *Book Ten*

All Kitten Aside *Book Eleven*
Oh My Roar *Book Twelve*

Raging Falls
Miss Taken *Book One*
Miss Matched *Book Two*
Miss Behaved *Book Three*
Miss Behaved *Book Three*
Miss Mated *Book Four*
Miss Conceived *Book Five*

FUR-ocious Lust - Bears
Fur-Bidden *Book One*
Fur-Gotten *Book Two*
Fur-Given Book *Three*

FUR-ocious Lust - Tigers
Stripe-Tease *Book Four*
Stripe-Search *Book Five*
Stripe-Club *Book Six*

Night and Day Ink
Bitten by Night *Book One*

Seduced by Days *Book Two*

Mated by Night *Book Three*

Taken by Night *Book Four*

Dragon Baby *Book Five*

Other Works

Wolf Fever

Fate's Wish

Wynter's Captive

Sinfully Naughty Vol. 1

Don't Drink and Hex

Hex Gone Wild

Hex and Kisses

Alpha Owned

Match Made in Hell

Alpha Geek

Contemporary Works

Lucky Chase

Their Second Chance

Club Duo Boxed Set

A Hero's Pride

A Hero Scarred

Wounded Soldiers Set

If you enjoyed the book, please consider leaving a review, even if it's only a line or two; it would make all the difference and would be very much appreciated.

Thank you!

64596262R00137

Made in the USA
Lexington, KY
13 June 2017